Where Bluebirds Fly

by

Brynn Chapman

To Michelle -
Happy reading!
Brynn!

Where Bluebirds Fly

Layout by www.formatting4U.com

All characters are from the author's imagination and have no relationship to anyone bearing the same names, save actual historical figures. They are not inspired from anyone known or unknown to the author and all incidents are pure invention.

Publisher: R. R. Hochbein

Acknowledgements

Writing may seem solitary…but when one is associated with the right group of people—it's nothing short of joyous.

My thanks to: MV Freeman, DT Tarkus, Robin Kaye and Marlo Berliner, Marcella Rose, Cathy Perkins, Hope Ramsay and Grace Burrowes.

Everyone at *Blame it on the Muse*, YARWA and especially Amy Atwell and her *WritingGIAM* sites. And Victoria Lea, for all her editorial guidance.

I'd also like to thank Ginny Crouse and Ralfe Poisson for assisting me with an accurate portrayal of Truman and Verity's synesthesia.

Dedication

For Jason: the best hearts partner around. Do not listen to them. We HAVE beaten them.

*finger can-can kick

For it was not into my ear you whispered, but into my heart. It was not my lips you kissed, but my soul.

— Judy Garland

Chapter 1

19th January 1692
Salem, Massachusetts

Some sounds you cannot forget.

They stay with you always, becoming part of you. They are as familiar as the creases lining your palms.

Some say what the eyes see, imbeds forever in our memories.

But *sounds* fill my head, late in the night, in my mourning hours-three refuse to die.

The sound of my mother's laugh. Low and resonant, like the church bell's peal on Sunday morn. To think on it too much would call madness into my soul. How that voice could lift me out of the blackness in my head and heart, threatening now to snuff the dwindling light of my hope.

The sound of my mother's screaming. It follows me down the path to sleep. Stays with me. My mother's hair, in blond waves, hangs loose from the Indian's pouch alongside my father's black and white locks. The gurgling, drowning sound in her throat tells me she's going, where I cannot follow.

The crunching snap of Goody Bishop's neck on the gallows' noose. The first to die under the charges of witchcraft.

No other visions of her remain, my eyes clamped shut at the sound.

My mother's tight grip and wild eyes plead with me to ease her pain. The blood from her scalped head floods her eyes. She doesn't blink it away. I think she knows she has only moments.

My little brother's chest heaves up and down as he clings to my legs. He's beyond horror—he's mad with it. His guttural childish-moaning splits my attention, ever so slightly. I must pay full attention to mother.

"My Verity," she croons. A crimson bubble of blood forms on her lips at the end of my name, and pops. "Do not forsake your brother, dear one. It shall not be easy. I love—"

John squeals like the devil himself has eaten his heart. *Perhaps he has*. My eyes flick up to behold the Indian. For a moment, compassion steals across his eyes, then they harden. He raises his tomahawk.

I reel at the revelry. My mind closes, my eyes slamming shut, refusing to relive the last seconds of my mother's life.

The *memory* is so vivid I feel the world twirl. I step forward, shaking my head back to life.

Sounds of the Salem Streets rush back like a crushing ocean wave.

Something strikes my shoulder, and I open my eyes, blinking against the sun.

"Verity Montague, one cannot stop in the middle of the fairway, child."

The goodwife's eyes say what her mouth won't allow. *You're mad. Your brother is mad.* The rumpled lips betray her fear, and her pity.

My present world rushes back with such alacrity, I drop the apple I've so carefully chosen. It rolls away into the milling crowd, and I give chase.

There's a tautness to the villagers; a thread of tension weaving through them. I see it in the hunch of my mistress's shoulders, the squint of my master's eyes.

My present, my responsibility, presses in. I hear my breaths, coming too quickly. Another woman notices, but her eyes quickly shift from mine.

A low drone of fret rises from my gut. *Not now. Go away.*

I know my brother John be somewhere in the crowd; late again, and likely in trouble.

Ever since the day of the Indian raid, a thick panicked sound thrums—embedded in my thoughts, like a swarm of hornets. I battle it, so I can try to live my life.

For me, the panic is a living, breathing creature. *A second self.*

It's hot, unrelenting fingers flick across my cheeks, as if my childhood memories are making a mad dash to escape, seeping out the back of my brain.

"Witch!"

My stomach leaps.

I spin toward the crowd, eyes darting, searching.

Somewhere a bell tolls.

My heartbeat matches my breath; two warring children, competing for my attention. My clammy hands grasp my bundle closer.

Where is John? Why can he never do as he is told?

You know why.

Because he is different from anyone I know. I am different, but I hide it. I *must* hide it.

I walk faster, dropping my eyes to the stares.

I mimic their countenance and cares, but inside, my heart throbs to its own abnormal cadence.

I do not love as they love—and what they deem important makes me laugh. If I dare to allow these thoughts to slip from my tongue, it shall be *I* swinging on the gallows. Followed by John.

A thick crowd gathers in the town square. I rush forward, scattering a flock of crows.

I weave in between the bodies, searching, listening.

My fear grows, and I feel my sanity tilting; tugging me to the edge of a deep, wide precipice. Awaiting in its depths, be madness.

"*Witch!* Where is the constable?'

I cannot breathe. *Please, please, no.*

The acccusations, again. They be after someone. I smooth out my face.

They must not know you fear. Show no fear.

"Witch!"

Fingers invade the air. Old hens and young children, all assuming the same accusatory pose. Each point at the cowering old woman in the center of the mob.

A bedlam of emotions crosses old Rebecca Nurse's face. Incredulity, anger, panic; then her twitching mouth finally chooses horror.

"Seize her! Examine her for the witch's mark!" Constable Corwin arrives, along with a bitter taste in my mouth.

I cover my ears in pain. The screams and shouts are deafening. Urging from all sorts; young and old, rich and poor. Once the condemning-frenzy begins, the enchantment will remain, till at least one be accused.

"She be a witch!"

"I saw 'er familiar the other night in the barnyard!"

Goody Nurse's tired, watery eyes open wide as the men approach. She freezes in mid-shuffle on the cobblestones. My stray, forgotten red apple rolls to a stop at her feet.

Her shaking hands pluck it from the earth.

Something clicks in my mind, like a rifle's cock. *John is near.* My head swivels all around, searching for him. *I must protect him, they hate him.*

The sides of my mouth spasm, breaking free of my mask.

I hear my mother's voice. *Save him, Verity.*

I must keep my wits, it means our lives.

I push my way through the crowd, hovering about the circle surrounding Rebecca Nurse. But my eyes keep returning to her.

I'm sick with helplessness. She doesn't deserve what they are about to do. Her wizened, healing hands cured John last winter, when no one else could touch his fever.

"I am not a witch!" The old woman's voice warbles, somehow drowning out the shouts.

The morbid fascination wins and I stand, transfixed, unable to look away. I command my feet to shuffle backward, but like some horrid enchantment, I am rapt.

Rebecca's crooked body trembles as Constable

Corwin yanks her arm.

She cocks her head to the side. The old dear is hard of hearing, and is most likely only catching snippets of the hurled accusations. Their superstitious eyes fixate on her.

My heart weeps to protect her, but what can I do? An eighteen-year-old servant girl?

Who will speak for her? Would they listen anyway?

"Your spectral self is accused of tormenting Anne Putnam, Jr., appearing by her bedside at night, beseeching her to sign the dark man's book! How plead you, woman?"

"Not guilty." Rebecca's eyes are bold, but her old voice cracks on the final word.

Corwin's eyes narrow.

"Oh, Goody Nurse," I whisper.

The whirrs of whispered voices are like a conspiratorial swarm of bees, closing the circle on her. *Tighter. Tighter.*

My skin itches with panic, I ball my dress into my sweaty, shaking hands; restraining myself.

The panic flows through the mob and I picture a beating heart—infusing the townsfolk with hysteria, powering the obsessive light in their eyes.

My mind rhymes, as it sometimes does, when I'm afraid.

Or insane. It's hard to tell.

The word drips from everyone's lips, the single condemnation…*witch.*

Witch.

Witch. Then, like a chant, the whole frenzied mob murmurs as one.

"Witch."

Two young women prattle beside me, shifting my gaze from Rebecca.

"Remember the old woman's dispute with Reverend Allen? Over where his land ended and hers began? Do you think this be why she is accused?"

The girl looks to be about my age. She wobbles on her tiptoes, her cheeks flushing with effort as she peers over the thick crowd.

"What do you think is Goody Nurse's familiar?" the other girl responds, too eagerly. Her greedy eyes shine with mischief, not fear.

Disgust rises in my nose.

"What is a familiar?" the terrified one asks, her gaze never leaving the mob.

"Why, it is how the witches travel. They take an animal's form, and force it to do their bidding." Her voice lowers, "One visited me last eve, a night bird *peck, peck, pecking* at my window. I think it was Goody Proctor." She stifles the giggle with the back of her hand.

"Are you mad?" I cannot stay my tongue. "This be not a game. Townsfolk are dying! Swinging on gallows hill from lesser whispers! Did you not see Goody Bishop hang?"

The giggly girl's gaze narrows; her eyes are black and beady. Dead, like a doll's.

"*You* seem a likely witch, Verity. Your looks are so odd! What *be* wrong with your eyes? One green as the sea, and one brown as dirt. Why don't they match?"

Heat floods my cheeks as rage reddens my sight. I suck in a breath. "You—"

The crowd roars, and we all three turn, transfixed once again.

"I said, examine her for the witch's mark, man!"

Constable Corwin spins Rebecca Nurse 'round, and with one practiced slash, rips open her dress. Goody Nurse's spine, curved and bent with age, is visible through the gaping fabric. I jam my eyes shut, cringing in mortification.

"Look there! It is the suckling mark!" The constable's finger juts at her lower back.

I spin back to giggly girl. "What be his meaning? The black freckle?"

She stares, eyes narrowing.

"Why, I have one here." I lift my sleeve.

"That is not unexpected, Verity."

Giggly girl's eyes darken with malice, her expression turning grave. "That be where the familiars come to suckle."

I yank down my sleeve. "Surely, you do not believe that claim?"

But it's certain from her rapt expression, she does. As does the daft one beside her. Not only do they believe it, they *revel* in it.

"I have seen evil in this world, but I do not think it takes the form of that kind, old woman? Who heals the sick?"

A more horrible revelation hits my ears.

"That boy be a witch, too!"

John.

The fear trickles down my thighs, pooling in my knees, buckling them. My heart trips in irregular patterns, knocking against my ribs.

I search the crowd for his face.

No fear. Show no fear.

I shove my way through the gape-mouthed throng. My eyes dart frantically from one grouping to the next. Finally, I see him and an exhale of relief escapes my lips.

He's easy to pick out. Every now and again, his arms and legs startle as if he's frightened. His limbs twitch as if each has an individual mind lodged inside.

He's like a puppet on a string, really. No control.

The familiar pain mutilates my heart; I press my lips tight and they tingle with the pressure.

They hate my brother, because his body disobeys his mind.

John tries unsuccessfully to blend with the crowd-his gangly arms and legs sprawling out like a newborn colt. He is all awkwardness as he sits alongside his painting and his liquid brown eyes widen in fear as the fat goodwife barrels down on him.

"I ask you, is it normal for the village imbecile to sketch like an Italian master? He's in league with the dark one, who grants him talent! The black master who afflicts the Parris children!"

My legs tense, yearning to seize him and run.

Fate suffocates me. *Where would we go?* We are captives to Salem Town.

I meet the fat Goodwife's gaze headlong.

She sees it as a challenge. Her meaty hands wring together, like a pugilist ready to brawl.

"And *you*! You have always been odd, I care not that you work for *the Putnams*!" She spits the name like a malediction. "Have the two of you been witches since your poor parents died in the Maine raids? They would be so ashamed, Verity Montague! You shame your father's house!"

White-hot fury incinerates my self-control at the invocation of my parent's name.

"Goodwife Churchill, you well-know my brother is sane as you. He is as innocent as the child unborn."

"Yes, that be what every accused proclaims."

The crowd's whispers rise. Snippets pop in and out around my ears.

"She is odd."

"Her eyes don't match."

"Why *do* his hands shake, so?"

Panic threatens. I long for my father.

The crowd is shifting from Rebecca Nurse, toward us, the new theatrical spectacle.

I search the crowd for support from someone, *anyone*, but I only find faces of fear or spite. All stare at John's drawing of Ingersoll's Ordinary. They wrongly assume the painting of the town watering hole is the source of the ruckus.

It's because he's damaged. I'm damaged.

"G-goody Churchill," John says, brown eyes filling. "I was only drawing, as I do every day when my chores are complete for the Putnams. M-might I gift you this one?"

"See! The imbecile tries to bribe me, to silence my accusations! I'll be having none of your tainted wares! Who knows what darkness lurks inside that painting? I'd sooner burn it than hang it on me wall. Call Corwin. Examine *both of them* for the witch's mark!"

My mind hums. We must escape before the shackles go on.

Fat Sarah Churchill whirls toward me again, as if

sensing my plan. "Behold the girl's eyes! I have never seen eyes as opposite as day and night."

She sticks out her bosom and paces before us, relishing the attention.

"Look at her—an orphan, no one to speak for her! No prospects, her life be doomed. And her i-idiot brother to care for!" Goody Churchill mocks John's stutter. "Of course she's taken up with the Dark Man. What other choice has she?"

A protective inferno rages. My fists ball, begging to pummel sense and bloody the nose of this *cruel, stupid woman,* who dares to taunt a soul like John.

"I did not take up with anyone! Or sign any book. I can't help the way I look." I shake my red, spiraling locks at them. "I was born this way!"

She shrugs and mocks, "Perhaps you were cursed from birth, Verity."

I force my hands down, twitching against my sides. The result is a shaking as wild as Johns.

John's hand squeezes around mine and I rally.

His eyes flick up and remind. *Do not show weakness; they smell it, like timber-wolves.*

I raise my voice, but it cracks, betraying me. "You are an orphan as well, Goody Churchill. Have you no compassion?"

John searches my face. A twitch flutters his eye. I smile at him. "As for my brother, I daresay this boy has more integrity in his big toe, than you possess in your entire person!"

The crowd rumbles at my challenge. A few laugh—anxious for a fight.

And then I see it.

My condemnation, flying toward me through the

air.

A bright bluebird.

The creatures will not leave me alone. They find me, wherever I am. It is completely against nature.

I've not done magic; *I know not* why they come. I am no spell-caster.

They shall be our undoing.

The bluebird circles, dipping into the crowd, trying to land on my shoulder. I duck and it misses.

People gasp, lurching out of its way as it swoops and dives. I hear more of them, calling to their comrade from the cornfield.

The circle tightens. *I cannot breathe*. The colors of their clothes blur, and I smell the man next to me. It's a musty, dank odor; like rotting greenery…or the prelude to death.

My mind screams and I crush my lips together to keep the terror in.

I hear footsteps. *They are come*. Corwin.

The bird manages to land before me, pecking the ground, hopping onto my boot.

Another goodwife speaks. "It's a bluebird. You know they be a symbol of goodness. Of hope; perhaps all is not lost?"

"Ha!" Goodwife Churchill scoffs.

This be our chance.

With one hand I grasp John's painting, flipping it under my arm, the other grabs him by the scruff.

"Goodwife Putnam is expecting us. Come John."

The bluebird leaves my boot, but hovers above, too close to be natural.

I avert my eyes and push John through the crowd. No one moves to stop us, but the murmuring recommences.

"Keep moving," I whisper into his ear. After a few, long minutes, I glance back. My breath whistles out. No one has followed us. They are too focused on poor Goody Nurse.

She's saved us once again. A lump forms in my throat.

The raised voices are fading as we move out of the town limits. The bird takes flight, across the cornfield. I know it will be back, though.

I whirl on John. "Do you not remember what I told thee last night? That queer times are afoot in the village? That only yesterday the little Parris girl was acting oddly, as was her cousin Abigail. People are twisted tight as overwrought mattress cords, what with the smallpox, taxes, land disputes…."

John's eyes squint as his attention dims. His gaze flicks to the forest and my patience wanes.

I know his mind recoils to a kinder, gentler place. But today…today he *must* listen. I understand his need to escape.

I often wish I could live in the stories I tell myself. Nevertheless, this world…is all we have.

"Are ye listening to me?"

"Hmm, yes. Smallpox. Dreadful."

I grip his shoulders, spinning him more roughly than I intend. It has the desired effect, however. His eyes focus, staring at me; his concentration renewed.

"You need to draw somewhere *alone.* Do not call attention to yourself in any way. And our secret—"

"Yes, you mean—"

My hand shoots over his mouth. "Speak of it to no-one. Since the girls have been working mischief with Tituba—"

"The Parris's slave girl from Barbados?"

"Yes, her," I say impatiently. "The girls have been having fits. *Convulsions, contortions*—seeing visions of people flying, perched on the beams of the church, and a man in black, urging them to sign his book. Mercy Lewis vexes me constantly for not going to meet with Tituba—but I refuse. She supposedly predicts the future. It's playing with fire, that is, in more than one way."

John's eyebrows dip in question, as they always do when I 'speak doubly'.

"You know that vexes me. At times, I can't discern plain speech, let alone when your thoughts have two meanings, side by side."

A wintry gust blasts our faces, and I shiver. I glance down, noting that John needs new boots.

Old man winter has come early this year. Redness glimmers in the night sky as the sun descends to bed. Spots of snow glisten in its amber cast, and a blustery crosswind from the north arrives with a cold that cuts to my marrow.

We automatically pick up our pace. We will catch it for being out so late. I see the Putnam's cornfield, now. The house is just on the other side.

A sound to my left. I stop dead, listening.

The corn rustles again; like a dog shaking off water.

The silky tops quiver as something picks its way through the rows. An animal? *The something is large.*

"What be that?" I step closer to the stalks.

"What? I did not see anything."

"Something moved in the corn. It was for but a

moment." My legs halt as if my feet have rooted in the soil.

An overpowering urge hits. Like a compulsive hook behind my navel, tugging me forward. "Let us go see."

John's eyebrows rise in vexation and surprise. "Verity, we might catch a switch already, we are so late? What's come over you? Keep walking. I be the troublemaker, not you."

I wrap my arms around my waist, trying to fend off the feeling. The tyrannical urge grips my throat, and it tightens. *Like needing a drink when you are parched.*

The Something in there wants me. Is it the infernal birds?

"What were you saying about the girls and Tituba-the witch slave?"

I start at his voice and rip my eyes from the field. "Witchcraft be not a game. I care not who I will marry, for I know the answer already."

John takes my hand, hauling me away from the rows.

The urge weakens with every step away from the cornfield. I suddenly feel the cold seeping above my boots and shiver.

John shakes my hand.

"Who will you marry, Verity. How can you know?"

I sigh. "I shall never marry. Too many women, not enough men. And I'm…different. And we're so very poor, John. What have I to offer? I'm already eighteen. Many girls my age have two children already."

John's expression is wistful, his eyes churning with turmoil. He quickly brightens. "Momma always said you were special, not odd. I believe Momma."

I spare John the retort hanging on my lips; that being *special*, might grant me a *special* walk directly up gallows hill.

My eye twitches as the noose's snap echoes through my head. The awful angle of Bridget Bishop's neck.

My whole body quakes.

"I think your eyes are pretty, Verity. No one else has them."

"If everyone could be like you, brother, the world would be kinder."

* * *

Anne Putnam Sr. glowers, her hands on her hips, as we stomp through the door. My mistress looks drawn and tired, the lines about her eyes just starting to show.

"Verity. Very presumptive of you and John to leave Mercy with all the evening chores."

Mercy Lewis, the other maid, smirks behind Goodwife Putnam's back. She pokes out the tip of her pink tongue.

Goody Putnam speaks again. "For punishment, John and ye shall do supper without Mercy, for three days."

"Yes, Goody Putnam."

I wait till the mistress departs, and set to my routine.

I steal a glance in the living room. Mercy whirls

in a circle, dancing with her broomstick. *Lost in one of her fantasies.*

I don't blame her, I have my own. But they don't involve dancing with a broom.

I duck back in before she sees me.

Mercy is pleased, no doubt. This will leave her extra time with Tituba, dreaming about her future husband.

I snort.

I carefully dip the bottoms of my skirt hem in the bucket water so as not to catch fire, just as my mother before me. Out the window, I see John's slim back lumbering toward the barn.

I tell myself a story as I shovel some coals from the fire's embers into the master's foot warmers.

"Ouch."

My fingertip sears with pain and I pop it in my mouth. I pull it out, half-afraid to look.

A small, angry boil rises on my index finger; my punishment for daydreaming.

Hoisting the warmer off the floor, I stomp up the stairs toward the children's rooms.

Tuesdays have always been red, but today the word blisters in my mind like brimstone. Monday is black, Wednesday-blue, and so on, through all the rainbow's colors.

My mother was terrified when I told her. "Speak of it to no-one."

Father later convinced her it was nothing infernal. Just another odd trait on my very long list.

Months, words, and individual letters illuminate in my head, all with individual hues. Like a fire made of driftwood.

As a result, my memory is extraordinary. I learned to read by four.

I have too many secrets. They weigh around my neck like a heavy millstone. I long to confess them. But it would condemn me.

I am alone.

I am different from girls my age, different from my masters. Different from everyone.

It's as if I'm a foreigner, incapable of speaking the language.

The loneliness is ever-present. An unwanted shadow, present both day and night.

I confessed once, when I was ten, to a houseful of children.

My eyes blink back the tears that threaten.

Time hasn't dulled their expressions, chanting, "Li-ar. Li-ar."

If I dared confess now, the name would be witch.

My colors are a memory aid; as much a part of me as my beating heart.

Echoes of mother's voice whisper, "Tell no one, Verity. Others will not understand."

I long for her.

The ache is unbearable. For her to look into my eyes and *hear me.*

No one sees me here. To some, I am a mere shadow, flitting about the edges of their conversations. To others, I am worth less than livestock. Something to be bought or traded.

Mother's voice again, reiterating, *Nothing good will come from it.*

This new country is set on uniformity, in Puritan thought and deeds. Calling attention to oneself is not merely discouraged, it's a sin.

I hear a knock on the door, downstairs.

I freeze instantly, the foot warmer banging against my leg.

I yank my skirt away from the flying sparks and recognize the harsh tones of Constable Corwin. The hornets revive, buzzing in my head.

My heart turns to granite, hardening with fear. "Mr. Putnam, we'd like to speak with you about one of your servants. The boy."

* * *

Present day
Clarion County, Pennsylvania
Penn's Orphanage for Exceptional Boys

"What? What's that bloody—?"

The landline beside Truman's bed was ringing. His eyes shot to the clock beside it, the digital numbers bathed the phone in a greenish hue.

Three a.m.

He wrenched the box off the nightstand, blinking stupidly at the caller I.D.

His teeth ground together in recognition. "Another emergency placement. Can't these people cut us a bloody break?"

A dog's shrill bark cut the night, startling him awake.

A chill walked down Truman's neck, blazing a trail of raised hairs. A crisp fall breeze blew in the open window, surreally swirling his dark curtains like an illusionist's cape.

Another bark.

Truman froze, hand poised above the phone receiver; his head alternating between the phone and the frantic dog outside. “Wot is he on about?”

He kicked off the down comforter and padded to the window. The phone silenced as the machine picked up and his assistant’s southern drawl began.

“You have reached Penn’s Home for exceptional boys…”

He hit the mute button and thrust his head out the old window frame. The familiar smells of barn animals, hay and half-finished apple cider wafted to his nose. A partially-stuffed scarecrow lay slumped over a bale of hay directly below his window; its yellow innards sailed up toward him in the rising storm wind.

Scanning the orphanage grounds, his mind ticked off potential hiding spots-the pumpkin patch, the cornfield, the barn? It’d be all-too-easy for someone to hide on the ten acres surrounding the orphanage.

He ducked his head back in, his eyes narrowed, checking the security monitor on the wall; its green blinking light reiterating the quiet scene outside…no breach in the orphanage’s security system.

Anxiety twisted his gut. He sighed, looking around for his jacket. He learned never to ignore his gut.

He felt so tired. Too young to feel this tired.

Did I bite off too much with this job? I mean, what other twenty-three-year-old has this responsibility?

His adoptive father’s voice retorted irritably in his mind, *How many people are a wunderkind, boy?* Tapping his crooked finger against his temple. *Will you use that mind for good or evil?*

He smiled wryly and shook his head. Despite being a million miles away, the man was still a force to be reckoned with.

The research paper on his nightstand reoriented him, its title glaring.

'Empaths and Synesthesia; A Case Study of T'

"Or alternate title, Truman Johnstone, The Modern-day Freak show."

He stared at the signatures beneath the title and squared his shoulders.

Ram Usman.

Soon to be head-shrinker and his very best friend. He must be, for convincing him to take this job at the orphange.

And below it, Dr. David Linkler; the aging pediatrician who'd opened the home, back in the 70's.

The paper, written about him, was to be Linkler's final scientific contribution.

The old man's visits were becoming less and less frequent as his legs weren't what they used to be, and slogging through the Clarion County mud took its toll on his rheumatoid arthritis.

Depressing the intercom button, he took a deep breath.

"Ram? Ram, are you up?"

"I am now." His friend's voice was thick, a little slurred. "What's up?"

"I heard something outside, the dog was going mental. Just wanted you to know I'm going to check it out. Better do the rounds—make sure they're all in."

"That dog is always mental. Truman, honestly, you're overreacting."

Though twenty-eight, Truman was convinced Ram had popped out of his mother's womb with a clipboard in his hands.

Born to psychoanalyze.

Truman grinned in the dark. He'd have to use that one in the morning, when Ram wouldn't rip his head off.

Pippin, the house Border collie, growled, her hackles rising into a furry black and white Mohawk down her back. She stood on her hind legs; her front paws clicking against the window frame.

Furry ears shot up, listening, and then lay flat against her head in disapproval as she stared out into the corn. Her upper lip retracted as she let out another low growl.

"Shh, quiet! I know, I'm going. I don't want every kid up and wailing."

He squinted and followed the dog's gaze as he stooped to snatch his scrubs from the floor.

A stark-white slip flashed in his peripheral vision and his head jerked back to the window.

What was that?

He jammed his head out, pushing the dog out of the way in time to see a sliver of white disappear into the cornfield.

He bolted— simultaneously wrestling a sweatshirt over his Occupational Therapy scrubs and took the back staircase two at a time till he reached the kitchen.

Flinging open the door, he sprinted, legs pumping, across the barnyard. A herd of cats scattered, mewling their protests.

A powerful tempest exhaled from the sky, blowing across the cornrows to shake their satiny heads.

He shivered as a prelude of lightning flickered overhead.

"Perfect. Hitchcockian, even."

Maybe I should've waited for Ram.

Intuition prickled and he chewed his upper lip, but forged ahead, ducking in and out of the sharp green leaves.

Thunder erupted in a deep baritone rumble. So close his insides vibrated.

He froze and cocked his head, listening.

He knew he was still safe; the crickets and cicadas sang in a round; their final summer sonata before the curtain call of fall weather. If danger was near, all would fall quiet, including the bugs.

He kept his eyes fixed on where the slip had disappeared. He ploughed through the stalks, not bothering to be quiet.

He flew, bobbing and weaving, deeper into the heart of the corn.

"Wish the maze were done. Watch me get lost in me own crop." He turned, checking his position with the farmhouse to get his bearings.

"Ridiculous. I shoulda grabbed the rifle."

He started as a high keening erupted—cutting the cicada's cut off, mid-note.

His heartbeat doubled.

A wail; then sobbing. It was definitely a woman, not a child.

His breath whistled out through his clenched teeth as his stomach unclenched a fraction.

It wasn't one of the kids. And Sunshine, well—he knew his assistant was the crying and, or, hiding type of girl.

Another sob and a hiccup. He tilted his head.

Where was she?

A woman stepped into the row ahead, barely visible through the maze of thick, green leaves.

Her head whipped around wildly as if confused. Her eyes were glazed as if she took no notice he was there.

She wore only a plain white slip. The wind gusted to reveal long, alabaster legs. Model legs.

"Wait, Miss? Are you ill?"

She slid back into the sea of green.

Domestic dispute? Runaway?

He hurried after her. His eye caught and locked on a snow-white calf.

His stomach contracted as if sucker-punched as he hurried toward her—ignoring the tiny slits of heat where the corn cut his cheeks.

The freakshow inside him began.

Emotive pulses rose off the woman's skin like steam escaping hot asphalt. Her emotions rode the waves, traveling to him and dousing him in their desperation; they slipped under his skin, making her pulse, his pulse. Her heartbeat, his heartbeat.

He swallowed. It was like a child's feelings, innocent and pure.

A color surrounded her body, as if a celestial being outlined her shape with an ethereal highlighter.

She was lavender, with a jagged red fear, seeping and pulsing in the center.

"What are you?"

Escaped mental patient? An ex-communicated Amish lass? Hallucination?

His mind tripped over the last one.

She doubled her speed, perhaps finally sensing him.

"Wait, miss! Do you need help?"

He'd grown used to his *peculiarities:* the way his instincts could discern a person's personality.

His mind worked, computer-like, to analyze a person's minute facial expressions, comparing them. He always knew when someone was lying. He was never wrong.

Ram informed him this was due to an over-wired limbic system in his brain.

He wondered what her name was…how did it taste?

His own was like mint. Ram had informed him the ability was termed *synesthesia*, or a mixing of the senses.

"Please, I won't harm you! Are you hurt? Just—wait!" Her foot slipped into the green. The sole was bleeding.

Hurdling a patch of flattened stalks, he reached the first circle of the corn maze. His woman in white, and she was indeed, a young woman, was now clearly visible.

Her chest heaved and the mystery girl bolted again, barreling down the path as if the devil were chasing her. Her old-fashioned ivory nightdress flowed behind her like she'd leapt from the pages of Wuthering Heights.

"Miss, stop! I won't hurt you! Please, you're bleeding!"

The figure reached the bridge, one of four placed in the cardinal directions in the maze. Lady in white sprinted up the northern-most bridge, leaving her bloody footprints in her wake.

Thick, auburn hair, in old-fashioned ringlets, bounced as she ran. The woman paused at the apex, and swiveled, with a slow, deliberate turn.

Their eyes locked.

His chest contracted like a knee to the ribs.

Her eyes were like…an open window. His emotions roller-coastered with fear—pain—longing and yearning.

He shook his head, refocusing. Now, they only looked terrified. And old—ninety year old eyes in a nineteen year old face.

He swallowed reflexively. They reminded him of holocaust photographs.

"Who are you?"

The tip of his trainer touched the first board of the bridge as her head shot to the right, breaking their eye contact.

Truman rushed her.

A low moan cut out of the corn's depths followed by a rhythmic, creaking sound—repeating in metronome-fashion. Like an auditory pendulum.

Her head whirled toward the sound and her fingers clawed her face.

"No!" she screamed.

Her thighs tensed and she bolted, tearing down the other end of the bridge. She leapt—and was airborne. And evaporated. Into *nothing*.

Truman stopped as the world shuddered.

How? His mind pleaded.

The air *liquefied* before him; it quivered, thickened, like heat on a summer's day. Poking it with his index finger resulted in a feeling reminiscent of thick treacle. He blinked. He couldn't see his fingertips.

He wrenched them out with a gnawing sensation chewing up his gut.

Unnatural, was the only word for it. The sticky feeling melted, along with the optical illusion of thickened air.

His insides quivered. His hand covered his mouth. He couldn't move.

Did I imagine it? A woman? One I created?

His pulse surged; its pounding and gurgling drowned out the windstorm.

His daily fear whispered. *Am I losing it? Is my childhood finally catching up with me?*

He'd done a psych rotation. He *so* didn't want to end up on the locked side of a ward. 302'ed. Incarcerated against his will. Because he was a threat to himself, or others.

Stooping, he touched the crimson outline of her footprint with his finger. A droplet briefly clung to the tip before dripping onto his trousers. If not for her bloody footprints, he'd have no evidence of her reality. Staring at her tiny feet, he felt…loss.

"I'm catching my patient's mental illness."

Chapter 2

They stood on the porch waiting for him, despite the hour. Ram's dark expression zeroed in as he exited the corn. His friend wasn't pleased. Three-year-old Anthony was cocked on his hip and Ram's foot was tapping.

Anthony wasn't crying. He stared up in awe at the dark skies, awaiting another thunderclap. Lightning flashed again, illuminating his pudgy, upturned face. Thunder growled and the skies opened, erupting in a deluge of sheeting rain. The droplets made an odd ticking sound on the corn leaves.

"Everything alright?" Ram's eyes shot behind him, looking for intruders.

Truman hurried toward the porch, sliding in the newly forming mud.

"You look terrible, your face is even more pasty than its usual Scottish shade."

"Thanks." *At least he's still joking.*

He didn't look Ram in the eye—they always revealed too much. He plopped down on the porch steps, slowly stripping off his dripping socks, trying hard to think.

He followed Ram's stare into the corn, unsure of how much to reveal.

Ram was finishing his PH.D in abnormal child psychology. Although they were best friends, this revelation would test that friendship. He was going to have to endure more of Ram's pleadings for additional testing. *Testing his mind.* He'd had enough tests, thanks.

Ram's analytical nature was reluctant to acknowledge anything he couldn't see or hold in his hands, and his mind was unable to wrap itself around anything extraordinary.

He, on the other hand, had seen badness be…the norm. So he reasoned, like the laws of physics, with so much bad, there must be good. He had no problem with faith or believing in the unbelievable.

His mind replayed the girl's image. *Time travel? Or schizophrenia? Psychotic break?*

Ram was researching a myriad of existential topics for his final dissertation; a subject to which Truman had been dealing out doses of relentless heckling.

Calling him, Dr. Strangelove. Dr. Spock. Dr. Who.

Ram had also tried, without success, to make *him* a psychology lab guinea pig due to his synesthesia.

"Snap out of it, True. You woke us at the crack of dawn! What did you see, man?"

Ram's coffee skin couldn't hide the black circles under his eyes. He was spent.

"I'm sleepy," Anthony added as if hearing his thoughts.

Wind blew sheets of rain onto the porch, wetting them. Truman retreated under the overhang, and Ram shifted the blanket to cover Anthony.

The light altered almost imperceptibly. Dawn was about to break on the horizon. An entire night lost to chasing a phantom.

His stomach clenched, replaying her long legs, her auburn hair.

A vision you seem to be rather taken with. In lust with a hallucination. Brilliant.

He cleared his throat. "Ah, another glorious day of dreary dark clouds. Typical Pennsylvania, reminds me of home. Let's go in—I'm drenched."

He opened the door without meeting Ram's eyes and walked toward the kitchen.

Ram stomped in behind him. "If you think this conversation's done…it's not."

Truman crossed to the counter, Ram's glare searing a hole in his back.

He pulled out the coffee decanter, filling it under the tap. Sleep would be impossible now. He stifled a yawn and started it percolating. His eyelids drifted shut, and he drank in the aroma while he waited. Hoping it would wake him by osmosis.

He heard Ram stomping up the steps, most likely laying Anthony back down.

His eyes strayed between the pocket doors, which opened to his Occupational Therapy clinic. He stared at the file cabinets where charts and summaries awaited.

He swallowed, pouring himself a cup of motivation.

A mountain of papers lurked in the drawer; past medical histories for new patients, arriving in—he checked his watch…four hours or so.

He sighed and took another slug.

He knew he was supposedly a *genius*, but right now, his impulses felt all of sixteen.

His mind screamed, over and over: *Jump on the motorcycle. Ride for hours. Ditch the job.*

But, he couldn't do that to Ram, not after he'd given him this opportunity. He'd put in a good word with the old doctor and convinced him to open the O.T. clinic as well.

Ram entered, the kitchen chair squeaking against the linoleum as he pulled it out. He plopped down across from him, scrutinizing. His black eyes tightened. "Out with it. You're hiding something. What did you see in there?"

Truman stared back. He rolled his eyes, resigned. "You're not allowed to think I'm a nutter; or give me any sort of *differential diagnosis.*" His fingers italicized the words.

"Oh, I already know you're a nutter. You don't need my signature to confirm that."

He flashed a white smile as he got up to fish a mug out of the cupboard.

Truman closed his eyes, bracing himself. "I thought I saw a woman in the corn. She was weeping and hysterical and she bolted when I called to her."

He opened them, monitoring Ram's response.

Ram's black eyes widened. "Should we call the cops?"

"Not unless you want *me* put away, leaving you and Sunny to carry on the insanity of this place alone."

"Why?"

"She was dressed in some sort of old-fashioned shift, like something from Plymouth Plantation."

Ram's eyebrows scrunched together in confusion.

He added, "You know, one of those 'history comes alive', places? Or even like the Amish down the road? And when she reached the end of one of the bridges in the maze…she erm—" He dropped his eyes and scrubbed his face with both hands.

"Yes?" Ram prompted.

"She…*dissolved.* To nothing." His gut twisted as Ram's singular eyebrow rose.

Thinking it was one thing, saying it out loud—quite another matter.

"Well, maybe she was a lost Amish girl?"

Ram recovered quickly, but not quick enough. He'd seen the brief flicker of panic twitch his mouth. *He's worried about my sanity, too.*

"I don't think so. Like I said, she disappeared." His gut performed another somersault.

Ram's face was both bemused and concerned. "Too bad I can't write prescriptions."

* * *

Salem

Tituba trudged across the snow-covered fields, intent on arriving at the Parris homestead before her master's return from the meeting house. Her husband, John Indian, kept time beside her.

"You know I'd never hurt ta girls," she whispered.

"'Course not. Dark times have come to Salem."

Tituba plodded as quickly as the deep snow allowed, her breath issued forth in puffs of steam. Her dark eyes glanced over her shoulder. The setting sun proclaimed their time was almost up.

Arriving in the kitchen, she sopped up the remainder of the snow from the floor as it trickled off her boots.

"Betty, Abigail, we are home!"

Her husband stepped in behind her, brandishing a few stocks of rye for her to examine.

"What is that black on the heads?" he asked, pointing to the tops of the sheaves.

"Do not think on it, we have more important things ta do. Goody Sibley says if we make the cake, it will block any *maleficia* working on ta girls."

Tituba left the kitchen and headed to their room. Standing in the doorway, she shoved a chamber pot into Abigail's arms and directed, "Make your water."

Both Abigail and Betty eyed her anxiously.

"You do it now. I might know a fix ta make you better."

Tituba returned a few moments later to collect her prize and headed back to the kitchen where John Indian awaited, stirring a mixture of rye bread on the table.

Dipping in the spoon, a few drops of urine dangled on the end of it before plunging into the batter below. Tituba's black hands worked the mixture into a cake, and she plopped it onto a grate, which would bake it in the fire's hot ashes.

Two frightened faces peeked around the kitchen door, watching her every move.

Removing the cake, she called to the dog, which padded over, wagging its tail.

"Here," she said, and its jaws engulfed the entire cake, devouring it with a single snap.

* * *

Verity

I slide closer till the hearth fire warms my back, hoping it will stop my shivering. The room feels too tight and close, as if Corwin's accusation has sucked out the air.

I try glaring back at the Constable, but my cowardly eyes keep stealing to Mr. Putnam, beseeching him.

The tension in the Putnam house *hums* like the air before a storm. My whole body is shaking, as if I've been deboned.

My nerves feel raw, exposed, like a lamb flayed for slaughter.

I breathe deeply. "I tell you there is nothing wrong with John."

My eyes sweep the room from Ann and John Putnam to Constable Corwin, whose unrelenting questions for the past quarter hour have beaten me to exhaustion.

Their faces remain stone. I try again.

"Nothing more than usual. You know he cannot speak his mind like others. He never has, since his birth—*this is nothing new*. Nothing to do with the Man in Black."

Ann Putnam crosses the room in the space of a breath and shoves her face so close I smell her sweat.

She spits, "Verity, it was at considerable cost we relieved Reverend Burroughs of you, John and Mercy after you lost your parents in the raids. We have treated you fairly. After all we have lived through with

Anne Jr., I would've thought you and John would have the sense to stay out of mischief! You have been meeting with Tituba, have you?"

"No, ma'am. I swear it!"

I struggle to swallow the lump choking my throat.

Anne's shrill scream rents the house, awakening a chorus of wails from the younger Putnams upstairs.

Accusations momentarily forgotten, all present fly out of the kitchen, up the stairs. I trail after them with Mercy and John hurrying behind me.

Reaching Anne's room, my stomach plummets to my boots.

My hands cover my mouth.

Her head *wrenches and contorts, wrenches and contorts*, cobra-like. Then stretches violently left, and *holds*.

Her blue eyes roll back in their sockets, revealing the whites, and she seizes in this posture-rigid. Her lips recoil in a painful grimace, revealing the pink flesh of her gums.

Her body flips from rigid to undulating; Anne's limbs quake and flail like river-snakes against the coverlets. Her jaw snaps shut with a sickening pop. The pink tip of her tongue juts out between her gnashing teeth and she clamps down with a howl of pain.

Blood-tinged spittle drips from the side of her slanted mouth and sweat pours from her forehead in tiny rivulets that darken her nightdress.

I ball my dress in my hands and feel John's frantic hand clutching the back of it.

"I can see her! I can see her!" Anne screams.

Her eyes stare past us.

"Who, who do you see?" prompts Anne Sr.

My mistress drops to her knees, clutching her daughter's hand.

Mercy cries, "S-she's looking into the spectral world!"

A gurgle bubbles in Anne's throat, slowly cutting off. Her limbs collapse to the bed and her breath rattles in and out in quick bursts and her eyes rove wildly beneath her lids.

Mercy grabs my hand and sobs into the back of it, her tears wetting my dry skin.

Constable Corwin's eyes find mine from across the room.

"Verity, you are sentenced to an hour in the stocks, for humiliating Goody Churchill in public. As for John—*we will be watching*. You best keep him in line."

Chapter 3

The undersides of my legs prickle and sting as if the wasps from my sick mind have migrated, feasting on a new area of my body.

The heels of my ankles are rubbed raw from the stocks. I wrench around trying to find someone, anyone.

A sharp burning makes me cry out; my skin rips open and a tiny trickle of blood cuts through the grime on my leg.

I taste the salt as my tears pass my lips, en route to my filthy neck.

I am nothing, an empty shell.

As if my real self abandoned this body and hides somewhere, awaiting the return of better days.

The hornets rise in my head. My depression is a dark blanket, attached and hovering at a million different points, to their invisible buzzing voices. They drop it, and it covers me.

The streets are clearing as people return to their homes to sup. Ingersoll's ordinary is within my sight and the sounds of eating and drinking fill the evening air.

My sentence was one hour, but I've been in the stocks since sun-up. Angry tears well again and itch as they cut down my cheeks. My hands writhe, useless in the stocks, as I struggle to wipe them away.

I hear footsteps approaching. I force my eyes up and my stomach roils. Goody Churchill approaches on the winding path in front of the stockade. I close my eyes on her delighted expression.

I think of John and pray fervently for his safety.

He depends on me to translate his thoughts, to decipher people's facial expressions, which often hold no meaning for him. He needs me. I must get back.

The footsteps crunch to a halt before me.

My eyes squint a blurry slit, but a burning *crack* across my cheek opens them wide.

Goody Churchill's bulk casts her shadow over me, hands on hips. Her fat face is a rumpled sneer and her laugh is rife with the unholy mixture of jealousy and condescension.

"Well, well, well. The tempest of your mouth finally landed you where you belong."

She steps closer, leaning down to whisper in my ear. Her breath is hot, laden with whiskey.

I wrinkle my nose, lurching away, but the stocks hold me prisoner.

Each word is velvety, smoothly-breathed. "I think you are a witch, just like that Tituba. I will see you and that fool brother of yours, hanged." Her lips peel back in a triumphant grin to reveal a line of rotted teeth.

She drags her finger beneath her chin as if an imaginary knife slits her throat.

I know Goody Churchill had been in the stocks only last fortnight for falling asleep in church…while drunk.

Something wet strikes the side of my head,

snapping it backwards as the pain clangs inside my skull.

My bottom slides off the bench, wrenching my legs in a painful twist as the stocks grind into my ankle's open wound.

The insects have control now. My mind hums, numb with their multitude. Swarming away with my sanity.

My stream of tears feels distant, as if belonging to someone else.

Silently, in my mind, I wail for my mother. This time, the pain won't be contained.

"M-mother, please, help me." Sobbing drowns my words.

Goody Churchill leers with pleasure; her cackle adds to the noise in my head.

A bright light fires in my dark mind-pushing back the swarm. It feels foreign; like a finger in my thoughts.

His green eyes. The man from the corn. Something inside me startles and wakes—long cold and dead.

I hear his voice, pleading with me to stop. His voice pushes back the dark.

"Ah, you're daft." She waves a dismissive hand and turns.

Realizing the fight has gone out of me, Goody Churchill retreats.

The footsteps recede with an occasional drunken hiccup. The image of him is fading. I want to reach out to him, to beg him stay.

Fear lets the cold trickle back into my heart. *Surely, the corn is enchanted. And if I return to him—I shall hang. For wanting him.*

I dare to open my eyes. A rotted corncob rolls on the ground beside me. My eyes flick across the fields.

The corn. The draw.

I laugh, and I hear the madness in it.

I shift my weight back and forth, trying to ease the searing pain on my legs.

The impossibility of my life presses on my chest, choking out my breath.

It is a vast void of repetition with no escape. Ever.

Rise. Chores. Eat. Chores. Teach John. Bed. Again.

With an occasional taunt or lashing thrown in, for good measure.

My vague memories of childhood are leaving me. My parents had not been wealthy, but they had been in love. And their love had sheltered us from hopelessness. They found joy in every task they undertook. I *need* those memories to stay. They are all I have.

"Please don't forget me and leave me till morn," I whisper. The thought of bears roaming in the nearby woods makes me sob harder.

More steps come into earshot. Squinting, I discern John's lanky figure, steadily loping his way toward me. I hastily take deep breaths, trying to compose myself. I must be brave.

The footsteps halt in front of me and I open my eyes, knowing they're bloodshot. My brother bestows a feeble smile, and I manage one in return.

My mother's final words echo in my head, the ones I'd blocked out before. "Take care of one another. The two of you are all that remains of us."

* * *

A screeching sound, which could only be one thing, met Truman's ears. He bolted toward the hallway.

"The bus is here five minutes early! Run!" he screamed up the steps— simultaneously flinging open the front door and giving the bus driver a singular index finger of 'wait'.

"Ram, we're going to miss it! I'll be late for patients and you for class!"

Ram skidded into the vestibule by the front door, brandishing five brown bag lunches and five coats. A stampede of footsteps thundered down the stairs.

Truman wrangled two blond boys into their coats. He bent, looking in their eyes. "Cade, you'll do fine on your test, stop fretting. Connor, you'll do fine with the music audition. Just take your time."

Ram finished with another pack of unruly boys and the quintet sprinted down the bricked lane to the waiting bus, which honked as it pulled away.

Truman smiled at the Honda Civic pulling up in front of the turnaround. Sunshine opened the back door and hoisted a bag of toys over her shoulders.

"What's she bought now? This clinic is already crawling with toys. I'm constantly stepping on them," Truman said.

Ram rolled his eyes. "I'm late. You have to call the Mensa people back."

Truman turned to look at him, his mind searching for recollection.

"The call, in the wee-hours of the morning? Remember?" Ram's face was impatient as he donned his black pea coat.

"In all the fuss, I totally forgot about it. We're going to catch it for that. We haven't responded within the time frame." Ram gave him a what-do-you-expect-me-to-do shrug, and took a step out the door.

"Never mind, I'll handle it."

Ram stepped off the porch and jogged toward his SUV, hopping over a stray ball. "Of course you will! That's why I chose you! Responsible."

He sighed. *Yes, if you only knew I'm trying to rearrange my afternoon so I can search the corn and stalk a figment of my cross-wired brain.*

"Oh, yeah. Responsible all right."

Sunshine crossed the yard and tripped. Her colossal bag banged off the sign, which read, *Johnstone/Usman Occupational Therapy Clinic, Specializing in Feeding and Sensory Integration Disorders*.

It rocked a little and she swayed, and accidentally smacked it again.

"Don't worry 'bout the sign—I can just buy a new one," Truman yelled as Sunshine trudged across the yard.

She lumbered up the steps, the heavy bag over her shoulders slumping her posture. Her red lips pursed.

"I don't want to hear it. If *I'm* bored with the toys, the kids will be too."

Truman ignored her. "We have precisely five minutes till the first one arrives."

She dropped the heavy bag to the ground and began extracting toys.

Striding into the clinic, he picked up a pile of charts and deposited them into Sunshine's already-full arms.

"Those are yours. See you at lunch."

He entered the clinic and strode to the desk; his own tottering pile taunted him.

"Right."

The redhead kept filling up his mind, distracting him.

He leaned on the stack of papers, closing his eyes. Her face appeared, perfectly clear, perfectly distraught, as he'd left her.

He licked his lips. He wanted to…smooth that expression away. And never see it mar her face again.

His watch beeped, his eyes snapped open. "Crap. I am completely mental."

Cracking open the chart, his eyes had time to scan the first few words, a diagnosis, when the clinic door opened followed by a child's wailing.

"Timmy! Come on, Timmy! You've been here a million times, when is this going to stop?" The mother's eyes held a desperate pleading expression.

Her fingers around the boy's wrist slipped as he hung there, a rag-doll suspended by one arm. She wrestled the four-year-old to stand.

"You are going to rip out your feeding tube. Please, I can't take another trip to the E.R. this week."

Truman plastered on a smile. "How's it going? Any new foods this week?"

Timmy quit his struggle, settling for lying face down on the floor, where he now rotated his arms in a frenzied rotary pattern, as if he were attempting a snow angel, without the snow.

The boy growled under his breath, voicing his displeasure.

"Well, he did manage a cheese puff the whole way through, chewed it and swallowed it, like you suggested. But when I tried the cracker…"

A violent retching sound exploded, clearly audible even from his facedown position on the floor.

"Tim…unbelievable. I can't even mention the foods or he gags." His mother sighed; her small exhale communicating a world of desperate exhaustion.

Underneath that hard exterior, Truman *felt* the waves of sorrow threatening to drown this brave woman; they were burnt orange. From Tim, a continuous, erratic pulse of amber fear emanated like a terrible Morse code.

"That's ok. You're continuing the bolus feedings through the tube? And I got the results of the swallowing study—he's clear to do the thin liquids from a cup, no aspiration."

When she looked confused, he added, "You know, no leaking into his lungs."

"Good luck with that," she choked. Her eyes glistened, despite being at this for months. She angrily pinched the bridge of her nose. "Sorry."

"It's okay. You know that." He winked.

A shiver of his past hovered around his thoughts, trying to find a way in.

Her expression rattled around in his brain like Marley's ghost, reminding him of his childhood.

When life is ghastly, everyday, anger may be all you have, the only way to stay alive.

Truman stooped, rolling the boy on his side. Lifting his shirt, his eyes traced the port for the gastro tube. The skin around it was healing.

"It's all cleared up around the edges. You can wait

outside, Judy. I'll give you the status report when we're done." She gave a relieved nod, and shut the door.

Truman's stared at the boy, who was unable to make eye contact. He would glance, look away.

Finally, he grasped the boy's chin, holding it there, waiting him out.

"Tim. Tim? It'll be fine, you know that." Finally the boy met his gaze.

Taking out the lotion, he squirted some onto his hands, and firmly rubbed the ointment into the boy's palms. Timmy gagged, and squirmed, pushing backwards. He signed the words, "All done."

"No, sorry lad. Not done yet, if you can't stand touching the food, you can't expect to eat it. I won't be there when you're twenty to help you feed yourself. C'mon, you can do this. If we get one new food today, I have a prize for you, ok?"

The boy closed his eyes, a solitary tear trickling out the corner. He extended his other hand to Truman to rub and gagged again before Truman even touched him.

Chapter 4

Winter, 1692

The dog growls, his frothy lips retracting to reveal yellowed teeth.

"The girls are subject to maleficia! Now the dog is afflicted, see, he ate the cake!" Tituba cries out.

The black dog's eyes stare sightlessly upward. He manages a wheezing, strangled bark, and my breath sucks in as I watch his limbs revolt. *Just like Anne Jr.'s.*

"Somebody help that poor creature!"

I'm standing in the snow, my teeth chattering from the cold.

I peer around the mistress of the house, Mrs. Parris, where she stands blocking the doorway. Her eyes, angry and afraid, chastise us.

"What are the pair of them doing here?" she rages.

I stammer. "W-We were sent by my mistress, Goody Putnam to—"

Mrs. Parris flies to the door, launching Tituba out of the way. Her face is livid red. "None of you should be here, this matter be private!"

Inside, the sound of heavy breathing clogs the air. We turn in unison toward it.

Betty and Abigail drop to the floor, twitching, seemingly in perfect mimicry to the dog's suffering. Betty's knee smacks the floor, and she doubles in half, expelling a violent eruption of sick down her shift. It pools about her, wetting the edges of her skirt. Its steam rises into the cool air.

Sobbing, she rasps, "Help me, Momma."

The girl's limbs quiver as if newly resurrected. They flutter uncontrollably, banging off her face as she attempts to cradle her head. "My head! My head be splitting!"

Abigail collapses beside her cousin. "I cannot breathe!" Her tiny hands circle her throat.

Hoarse chokes, punctuated by sobs, rack her chest with every inhalation.

Mrs. Parris is disintegrating. Her eyes are wild, like a trapped animal. "Oh-my-girls-oh-my-girls, Satan be gone from our house! Tituba fetch Reverend Parris!"

I vault past Tituba and drop to my knees beside Abigail, cradling her to my chest. Beside us, Mrs. Parris sops the sick off Betty's soiled dress.

Her face…will haunt my dreams. Her fear is eating her alive, like the hornets devouring my mind.

"Tituba, go!"

Tituba breaks from of her frozen position on the floor, rushing out the door.

Out the corner of my eye, I see John step through the doorway. His eyes full of the dog quaking at his feet. Tears flood his cheeks as he bends, hand outstretched.

He's drawn to animals, more than people. People hurt him, taunt him. Animals only love him.

"Do not touch it, boy! Are you mad? The creature is beyond our help now!"

Reverend Parris ploughs into the kitchen, Tituba and John Indian following in his wake.

His face is tinted purple, his hands clench at his sides, as if he restrains himself from throttling me. *As if this is all my doing.*

His finger stabs the air. "Twice now, in *your* presence, these afflictions occurred. Were you not just released from the stocks some hours ago for suspicion in Anne Putnam's fit?"

A muscle twitches below his left eye.

I cringe at his hatred. Inside the hornets snicker, buzzing to life.

His eyes flick to the dog. "Devil-dog. It shall be hanged." I stifle a sob as he launches forward, sweeping the animal into his arms.

It whimpers a low, baleful sound. The dog's tongue lolls out, pink and frothy, from between its teeth.

"Oh sir, m-must you hang it?" John says. His hand claps over his mouth, astounded at his own forwardness.

John's eyes plead. "I mean, he looks ill."

"*Ill?* Don't be naïve, boy. Dog's may do a witch's bidding, same as any man. This animal is condemned. It be a familiar."

I hear Tituba whisper, "But it ate ta cake." Her shoulders slump in defeat. She's only trying to help.

Under my arm, Betty quivers again. Her eyes jiggle to and fro in their sockets, then glaze over. She stares off as a vacant expression settles over her face. Doubling over, she clutches her stomach and writhes.

Her scream raises the hair on my neck and sours my blood. John's hands fly over his sensitive ears.

"I see her—she's pinching me!"

"Who?" Reverend and Mrs. Parris exclaim together.

"It is Tituba!" Her limp finger directs blame. "She's in her spectral form!"

My head snaps to Tituba. She shakes her head. Her tortured eyes overflow with tears.

"No. I would *never* hurt ta girls."

* * *

Truman checked the pocket-watch; a gift from his father the day he left Scotland. Guilt prickled his conscience; he needed to call him. Better yet, go and see him. The old man's words replayed in his mind, "Don't know what you expect to accomplish over there. Nuthin ya' couldn't do here."

His eyes flicked to it again. 3:45 p.m.

He had fifteen minutes till the pediatric stampede.

Pulling the bit of paper from his pocket, he punched in the numbers on his cell and stepped out onto the porch.

Sunny passed him, and he held his finger to his lips to shush her.

Her red, manicured nails twiddled goodbye as she crossed the yard to her car. He watched her exit the estate and turn onto the main road. She stuck her tongue out before gunning it, spinning gravel.

He shook his head and smiled. *She's a trip.*

The phone rang on and on. The corn rustled, and his eyes searched, sweeping across the center. The green undulated in linear trail; as if something was wandering, cutting across the rows.

A wave of color appeared, hovering over the corn tops, about a mile in.

Sweat immediately dampened his collar.

His heart throbbed, hard and fast. He looked around for help—but he was alone.

Intuition prickled.

His lips parted as it struck. *The pain.* It was exquisite, acute—a migraine of emotion, cutting him down.

A lightning bolt of suffering bored his subconscious—searing into his brain, into his own desires.

He stumbled, grasping for the porch railing.

The sensations tumbled in, rolling from the south end of the field, wave after wave of purple and black.

Is it her, the girl in white? Is she in danger?

The hand holding the phone dropped to his waist. He looked around madly, seeing nothing as the panic won.

A primal urge to protect her, to find her. To save her, consumed him.

A bell tolled.

Truman cocked his head, listening intently.

His breathing staggered.

Silence again. It was only once. *The closest church is twenty miles away.* He paced, vaguely aware of the phone ringing on speaker.

I am losing it. Medication, do I actually need medicated?

The phone rang endlessly.

"Why isn't the bloody MENSA voicemail picking

up?"

He scanned the corn as a new crest of emotion lambasted him. This one, a scarlet tide.

It *ebbed* and *receded*, *ebbed* and *receded.*

His stomach clenched and calmed in sync with its moving presence.

A low cadence weaved between the undulating colored waves; like an audiovisual fabric, assaulting him. The beat was threatening.

He bit down hard on his lip, tasting blood.

Suddenly, with a barely audible pop, the wave sucked backward, and was gone.

He blinked, confused.

A shocking blue sea had taken over the field. Another wave?

He squinted. *Birds?*

Bright, azure blue birds sat atop the corn. Hundreds of beady-black eyes stared, as if watching him.

His nostrils flared. "Go away."

As if hearing, they erupted in a blue blanket across the sky.

The flock swerved as one body and swooped down once again, in a blue explosion to the southern-most part of the maze.

His heart skipped a beat.

He felt her, the girl, when they were near. And now.... Emptiness.

"I-I...."

She made him *feel*, with a singular look. Something he'd strategically avoided since childhood.

No attachment, no pain.

His empath-extra-sense had read her heart like an

open book.

And worse—he had glimpsed what was *possible.*

Seeing her, experiencing her feelings, was like breathing for the very first time after a life-long emotional suffocation.

He ground his teeth together. "That is bloody ridiculous."

But, the draw was real. Even now he could feel it—its intensity crippling; like being separated from the other half of your mind…your heart.

What's wrong with me?

"You don't even know if she's real. Or something you created."

The yearning was unbearable.

Ram stepped onto the porch. He started so hard the phone flipped from his hand. He juggled it, caught it and shoved it back against his ear. The low-drone of the endless ringing continued.

Ram looked at him; no, *examined* him. Obviously worried.

Truman searched the yard, but no car. The git must've used the back entrance.

Ram picked up as if their conversation had not been separated by eight hours of work.

"That would make sense, actually. If she's a specter, there's no way you will have to commit, right? It's the perfect relationship for you. Even better than an Amish lass," he said in a pathetic attempt at Truman's accent. "You won't have to convert."

Truman covered the phone with his hand. His heart was still skipping. He tried to joke. "Dude, I don't know what continent that was supposed to be from, but it definitely wasn't mine. India meets

Scotland is completely lame."

Ram stepped into the house, but poked his head back out a second later. "Also, you might want to quit talking to yourself. I don't think the state will look kindly on granting us wards if the fearless first-mate is certifiable."

"You're one to talk—"

But the phone finally stopped ringing, and a woman's voice picked up. "Hello, this is Stephanie."

"Hi Steph, it's True Johnstone. I'm returning your call for the emergency placement the other night."

"Yes, well, you're aware *when* I called."

"I apologize. We had a wee bit of an incident, and then patients started coming, and this is the first chance I've had…."

And I'm completely mental. Experiencing love at first sight. Or possibly schizophrenia.

"Well, I saved him for you, because I don't think anyone else can handle him."

Truman closed his eyes, dipping his head backwards.

That means a family history like Running with Scissors.

He took a deep breath. "What's his story?"

"He's five. He's non-verbal. We think from the trauma."

"Define *the trauma*."

He checked his watch, and headed into the clinic—he was running out of time. He scribbled notes on a piece of notebook paper.

"His parents died in a fire. Arson. The police suspect…him."

"How could a five year old willingly—"

She cut across him. “He was I.Q. tested at head start. It’s at 145. He’s a bona fide genius—I knew you’d relate. The boy’s been writing at a fourth grade level and doing multiplication for a year already.”

“He communicates by writing?”

“Yes, and some sign language.”

Truman sat, his head slumped to the desk, and he gently rapped his forehead against its shiny surface. The wood was cool against his sweaty face. “And…I know there’s more. Don’t spare me.”

“He has a feeding tube, his parents were from the low income housing section, and we suspect neglect at best, at worst—abuse.”

“Always I think you can’t surprise me, yet, you always do. It’s a gift, really.”

“He has sensory problems too. Can we bring him over tonight? He’s an orphan now, True, like you were.”

I swear she uses that to manipulate me. Especially when she knows we’re full.

Ram stepped into the clinic, joking demeanor evaporated. His black eyebrows furrowed and he cocked his head, mocking Truman’s posture. He shrugged his shoulders in question.

Truman sighed and put a finger-gun to his head. And pulled the trigger.

The bus beeped outside, and Ram flew out the door.

“Yeah, fine. But he’s absolutely the last one. We’re full now.”

Chapter 5

7:45 a.m.

"This is ridiculous." Truman yawned into the back of his hand, and gave the house, and his window one final, longing glance— thinking of his bed.

He turned into the rising sun, and stopped dead in the break in the corn, letting it warm his face.

Ram set aside the time for him…for his own personal therapy; it'd be wasteful to squander it. Which was hilarious as he'd refused counseling all of his life.

He shook his head and resumed walking. "What if I don't like reflection? What if I prefer denial?"

Then you'll be perpetually screwed up, the Ram-voice inside his head chastised.

He much preferred the chaos of the house, where there was no time to think.

His past hovered over his sanity like a stalking, mental, serial killer—just waiting for him to lower his defenses.

Like I'm supposed to do now.

He walked without direction, staring at the bright green and yellow-flecked stalks, noting the corn hadn't ripened.

Mud squished under his trainers. The notebook in his hand felt leaden; it captured the ghosts of his past, housing them in a scribbled limbo.

He loved and loathed it simultaneously.

Its old, leather-bound contents began with the ramblings of his thirteen-year-old mind, right up to last week's painful recollections.

He'd been journaling long before Ram prescribed he do it. But now, maybe because it was a 'mandate' to his therapy, it felt forced and uncomfortable. Like someone sewing a scratchy decal onto a well-worn, favorite shirt.

His foot struck wood, sending a pang through his toe.

I'm at the North Bridge.

Once his favorite spot, he'd been strategically avoiding it—since his longing-induced hallucination, had chosen it as her haunting place.

He sighed and walked up to the apex, plopping down.

He cracked the journal open, staring at the evolution of his handwriting. From boyish scrawl to…worse, really.

He ground his teeth together, and pressed the pen to the paper.

~ ~ ~

Am I happy? I'm not really sure what that is? I've found a place to be, where I'm needed, for the first time—so I guess that is progress.

~ ~ ~

A crackling sound cut through the early morning calm. The walkie-talkie on a nearby stalk buzzed to life.

"Truman? Can you hear me?"

He jogged down the planks to the stalk, depressing the button. "I'm here. What's going on?"

"You have an add-on patient at eight a.m. You better get up here."

"So do I get demerits for not journaling?"

"Shut it." The crackling stopped as Ram flicked off the talkie.

He ran back toward the house, smiling in smug relief.

* * *

The stalks are dying. Soon they shall no longer hide me.

I glance back at the Putnam house, knowing I have only moments, the few stolen ones, alone. I crave quiet and solitude—impossible in a house full of children, masters and John.

I stare at the setting sun, thinking of Momma. The tears still come. Not because of the pain. It's not sharp, but an old ache, accepted but constant, like an old one's rheumatism.

When I'm alone—my circumstances overwhelm. Like a recurring nightmare. One that comes every night, that I must endure, step by excruciating step—till morning's light comes to relieve it.

But for me, there shall never be a morning.

I hear the whisper of the hornets, and melancholy's deep pressure settling against my chest.

I stop, sucking in a breath. The bridge?

It has returned. The night I saw him….it appeared then, beneath my feet without warning.

My eyes return to the household. I cannot see it, the corn is still high—so they cannot see me.

"Is this the work of the Man in Black?"

My heartbeat doubles in time with my breathing.

A book, face-open, lies at the top of the bridge.

I bite my lip. Is this the dark book everyone in Salem has been so afraid of? The one the Dark Man makes them sign, to pledge their allegiance with their souls?

"Be brave. If it is, you must turn it in. It is your responsibility."

My courage seems to liquefy, pooling and weakening my knees. I step onto the bridge, balling my dress in my hands. I trip the last step, falling on all fours to stare into its open pages. What if the words bewitch me?

My eyes scan the page and I drop to a sit. I gently gather the book into my hands, gaze racing left to right, left to right as I digest the words.

~ ~ ~

I thought of ending it today. I am so alone. Alone with only my abnormalities for company. This is the fifth foster placement. I overheard them whispering about me tonight. About how I'm different—too different to stay with them. They already have 3 foster children—all average. 3 girls. I'm the first boy. I've tried not talking, to pretend to be normal. I fixed their computer. Instead of being grateful—they stared at me like the freak that I am. I watch her hold the little ones. I've never had a mother hold me. Never tell me everything will be alright—even if it's a lie.

~ ~ ~

Tears cut through the grime on my face. "Never

to know a mother's love. That be dreadful."

When the memory of that love is the only reason I rise in the morning. And I have John. Who's difficult, a constant worry—but who's my flesh and blood. Alone. I thought I was alone. But this writer—he is truly alone. My eyes dart back to the page.

~ ~ ~

If I can just survive two more years...I can become an emancipated minor. Get grants and go to college. And I'll be alone, again. But free.

~ ~ ~

"Free."

The word cuts. The impossibility of it. *I will never be free.*

My heart aches for this boy, man…what is he? Where is he? So many words I do not understand?

My heart's been chopped into sections, reassembled, and sewn back together. But it'll never beat properly; out of time and disorderly.

That is precisely what his words say to me.

Far off, a voice calls, "Verity? Where are you?"

Mistress Putnam.

Fear, and a longing I have no right to, fill me in equal measure.

I open my pack which contains John's tutoring utensils.

I hastily pull out the ink and bite my lip and touch the quill to the parchment and cringe—praying the Dark Man does not appear.

* * *

6:30 p.m.

"I will be back," Truman called over his shoulder, already two steps into the corn.

"Where are you going?" Ram's clipped tone echoed behind him.

"What are you, my wife? I forgot to do something. I will be right back. Ten minutes, tops."

Truman picked up his speed, angling in and out of the rows. He used to run track in high school. He didn't have a choice. The coach saw him sprint once…and that was all it took. The man was relentless.

He was fast. Still was.

The bridge arrived in no time. He felt better when he ran. His mind cleared and uncluttered of all but his breathing.

He let his breath exhale in relief. The journal was still there—and it hadn't rained. He looked up at the brooding sky.

Yet.

He sprinted to the top, swiping it up. Something caught his eye. A corner was turned down. He never did that—the book was so old it couldn't take the abuse. It had survived a journey from Scotland to the States, and five foster homes.

He opened the page. His eyes widened and he cocked his head, disbelieving.

"What the…?"

He collapsed to the bridge, legs crossed.

He turned the pages, faster and faster, shaking his head.

His finger followed along the loopy handwriting, page after page of it. Someone else's words…written in his journal. Someone had written in his journal.

~ ~ ~

It's as if I'm living in a tale my dear mother told me as a child, before bed. Finding this book. Writing my fears into it—perhaps they will leave my head, now. Dear writer—I understand alone. My dear family...was murdered.

~ ~ ~

A tear must've streaked the ink, as the next few lines were blurry, unreadable. This made him anxious.

What did they bloody say? What is this?

He glanced up, half expecting to see one of the high school boys guffawing in the corn. But no-one. Dead calm.

He quickly flipped the page.

~ ~ ~

I have a brother with me still. I understand alone. The worst for me, is the time between awake and asleep. Where I have no control—and I don't know what is real. I feel death looking for me, then. Trying to convince me to come along, after all, my parents await.

So, dear writer, I'm listening. I know these words to be bold, and unconventional—to speak so plainly to someone I know not.

But it's as if I may confess my heart here—in the pages of your powerful book. And your words are powerful. Trust when I say, I am thinking of you, at this very moment, carrying your words and thoughts with me—like a talisman against the dark.

~ ~ ~

Truman blinked, felt the wetness. His mouth still hung open—he wasn't sure if it was the shock of the wordy revelations, or that he was actually crying. He hadn't cried since he was what…twelve?

He squinted. He couldn't see the page anymore. It was too dark.

"Oh my gosh, it's too dark. Ram is going to go ballistic."

He tore off the bridge, heading through the rows.

He looked down at the journal.

He was torn. Ram was already going to be so ticked—he'd likely ignore him for days. He'd have carried out most of the nightly rituals without him.

"So dead."

He reached the corn's mouth, and stopped to stare at the orphanage's wraparound porch, and back to the journal.

"He's already furious. What's five more minutes?"

He darted into the barn, and to the pile of junk stacked at the back beside the hay bales.

He rooted around, till he finally found it. "Yes."

A dirty, plastic container, with a lid.

He grabbed a pen from the miscellaneous charity pile, and cracked open the journal. He hastily scribbled a message, and jammed the lid back on.

He darted to the barn-door, back out into the corn, toward the bridge.

This was one time his speed was actually coming in handy.

Chapter 6

Who are you? Where are you? Your words…well, I could've written them myself. I am so very sorry about your parents. But they obviously taught you well—your love for your brother shines in every word. I, too, am listening. What could I do—to help you? What is your name?

~ ~ ~

I'm very frightened, writer. There is something wicked happening in our town. People are being accused, and hanged. And—well, not only am I different on the inside, I am different on the outside. My eyes—are unmatched. People have taunted me for as long as I can recall. Today—I heard their whispers as I passed by. So many names for my brother and I.

~ ~ ~

Reader, hanged, really? Are you serious? What matters, is who you are. And by your words, it's evident—you are a pure, pure soul. One undeserving of all this unkindness. I—I never knew my mother. She left me, at an orphanage. Truth be told...I've never known a home. So, although your home is lost—keep it close to your heart—to carry you through—when these others ridicule you.

~ ~ ~

Writer, I have not heard such kind words, for so many years. I hope, good sir, you find your home. Everyone does have one. But sometimes, it's not within four walls. But within your heart.

...I feel as if I live in my head. In my own dream world. Never confessing what I really feel to anyone. I feel I'm on a dangerous edge. That I can no longer contain my thoughts.

~ ~ ~

...I live in my thoughts too. No one I know...thinks like me. Sees the world as I do.

Reader. I must meet you. I have not dated anyone...in years. I never seem capable of small talk. How do I start a conversation? Hi. I am a complete hot mess? We've already shared the deep dark recesses inside...I feel I must meet you. Please.

~ ~ ~

Writer. I don't know if that would be proper. But I must admit—I want to. I find myself thinking of your words all day long. I cannot focus, and find myself wishing. Wishing too much, for too many impossible things. All of which concern you. A man I have never laid eyes on.

~ ~ ~

Reader (what is your name!) nothing is impossible. Well, some things are...but one must hope. Hope is at times, all we have. And as to convention—I have lived my whole life on society's fringes. Convention is for the weak.

~ ~ ~

...her blood...was all over my hands. I still see it there—in my dreams I scream and scream, but it won't wash off. The stain is permanent.

~ ~ ~

...the second orphanage was bad.

~ ~ ~

Tell me. I'm listening.

~ ~ ~

...there were cockroaches, under the covers. They cut a hole in the second floor, and put a burn barrel beneath it—to keep us warm. It was so cold. I wore my boots to bed.

~ ~ ~

Oh, writer. I wish I could be there. To hold your hand.

~ ~ ~

We must meet. Tell me when.

~ ~ ~

I-I've never done anything...improper. But...yes, I shall meet you.

~ ~ ~

Meeting won't be wrong. I promise.

~ ~ ~

I will have to come at night. At dusk?

~ ~ ~

On the top of the bridge?

~ ~ ~

On the top of the bridge.

* * *

Verity

I stare at the sun. Its orange glow just visible over the tops of the corn. Only for a moment, and it's gone.

The night birds are calling as I reach the bridge.

My heart falls. I look around, past the bridge, through the rows. No sign of him anywhere.

I hear my mother's voice, scolding, *Verity, you do not know this man. Or his family. He may steal you, hurt you.*

"No. I don't think so Momma."

My heart beats hard, and I wish, again. I care not if he is old. Older than even my master. Or if he's ugly as a troll. It is who he is. I just wish to talk to him, to be near him.

I stand on the bridge, holding my breath, still turning in a circle, searching.

My boot kicks something.

The box.

The strange, clear case that houses the journal. It was not there a moment ago. I shiver, still not convinced this is not the work of the Man in Black.

I crack it open.

~ ~ ~

Where are you? Why didn't you come?

~ ~ ~

My stomach flips. I hastily scribble in the book, place it in the container and kick it.

It slides over the top…and is gone.

"Where are you?"

I hear his voice, just like the first day in the corn. It sounds far away. Like it's floating upwards, out of a deep well.

"I'm here!" I flinch, and quickly turn as a flock of birds—those odd bluebirds, take flight.

I hold perfectly still, entranced. There are so

many, for a moment the sky is blotted out.

"I can't find you." His voice is closer. Like he's beside me.

"Keep talking. I can hear you now." I bite my lip. "Your voice is lovely."

I hear the smile in his. "You stole my line."

"Verity! Where are you, girl?"

"Oh no, my mistress is calling. I must go. I am so sorry. Please—can we try again?"

"Your mistress?"

"I have to go. Write me soon."

Chapter 7

John crawls into his bed whilst I perch on the edge. He slides beneath his blankets, and looks helpless and innocent. Even in the relative safety of the Putnam house, my fears resume. My hands flutter almost as violently as Abigail's. I sit on them so John won't see. My mind keeps returning to the pitiful dog, and how every day seems one step closer to the noose. For everyone.

"Are you warm enough?" I try to force my face into calm.

John nods, but his color is pale, his eyes, dim.

His hope is fading. I don't know if I can raise his spirits, my own be so melancholy.

"I am so sorry about the dog."

He holds up his hand, shaking his head. He does not want to talk about it.

"I understand."

Some things, no amount of talking will heal. Only time. He feels pain so acutely.

I drop my eyes to stare at my hands, thinking of the endless taunts he's endured. Since he was old enough to walk-lope, really.

Monsters, all monsters, they are.

"Do you want me to sleep with you?"

"No. I will be fine. I will see you on the 'morrow."

I stand to go. His hand catches mine as I turn away.

I face him again.

"I love you, sister."

I blink back the tears. He needs me to be strong. To *believe* I will make him safe.

A silly, weeping girl cannot protect him. A fierce, consuming, motherly instinct roars in my chest. Ignorant people.

It is *they* who are stupid. Who cannot understand his paltry words don't match the depth of intelligence inside his head.

I seethe, thinking of their stares. Through condescending eyes. Considering him *less* than them. Indeed, he is so much *more*, than anyone I've ever met. I swallow my hatred, and unstick my throat. "I love you, too."

I walk to the doorway, not seeing. Yearning for the past has me by the heart now, refusing to let me be. I turn to face him, repeating the words we've heard together when home was *home*. And our beds and minds were safe. "Till the sun doesn't rise and the moon doesn't shine, love."

His responding smile finishes me. My breath stutters.

Shutting the door, I press my cheek against the wood. Both hands cover my mouth, squeezing my cheeks. My chest shakes silently. I feel the wail building—I will wake everyone.

Something snaps inside. I fear it's my self, my sanity?

I feel detached, like my insides fight to separate my soul from the cloying, sodden pain, infecting my heart.

Blackness crouches on the edges of my sight. The halls waver, dreamlike.

Would anyone love John if I passed?

A life without love. Perpetual loneliness. *Why live?*

I long to be with my parents, even in death. When I was with them, I felt whole, a person deserving of love.

Every day in Salem since their death, is muted, every breath, like drowning. I shake my head. No, he needs me. What if the constables come for me?

Please, God, let someone else love him, keep him safe. Oh, please let it be so.

The loneliness; I can no longer tolerate it. And it is possible to be lonely in a crowded house, like this one.

I stare at my hands, the burns littering my fingers. They've become infected before. People die from such a little thing. The fear of leaving him alone, unprotected, chokes me, and I gasp.

I am whispering and pacing and I cannot stop.

"No coin. No family. So, incredibly, unforgivably different. There is no hope."

I must leave. The need is unforgiving, and primal. Like the need to breathe. I flee, passing bedroom doors, where the quiet sounds of snores fill my ears.

A revelation hits. My writer, and the man in the corn…are the same?

Suddenly I must know.

Reaching the kitchen door, I fling it open, pelting

out into the freezing night. The moon shines so bright, the whole of the barnyard is bathed in its luminescent glow. It's like walking in another world. A black and white one.

New, white snowflakes buoy on the night air, hovering and shimmering in the moonlight before swirling down around me. The remnants of the corn, partially rotted but still standing, call me.

I feel the draw. And somewhere, music starts. Strange music, with a woman's voice. Sad, and longing.

I listen harder. I can make out some of the words. "Lullaby…trouble…bluebirds?" I whisper.

Music, outside? How? From where? Bluebirds? Does she summon that flock?

I hear *writer's* voice again. Calling me from the dark.

I've tried to convince myself it's a dream. The notes. His words. That he is a beautiful angel, come to coax me from despair. But the pain in my foot, where I'd cut it in his field, now stings, as if to prod me forward.

"It is folly. I am enchanted."

A small voice inside whispers, *Then so be it.*

I am running, flying toward that bridge.

No one, besides John, has looked at me that way since Maine. Since…*say it.*

"Since the raids." I vault over the rotting leaves, their musty smell wrinkling my nose. "Since we put them in the ground."

I hear the music rise in time to my footsteps. The sound is like none I've ever heard. Many instruments, layered upon one another, like the overlays of blankets on a bed.

My legs pump till they burn. I laugh, exhilarated by the wet kiss of the snow hitting my face. I am shivering wildly, and I don't care.

I picture him in my mind, and it blazes with light. A light I was certain was dead. Blotted out with grave-dirt, buried forever with the love of my parents.

My boot strikes wood, and the pain in my foot sings.

I stare down in glorious triumph at the bridge.

The Bridge of Evanesce, or fade-away, I realize I've named it.

I grasp its railing in my shaking hands. He's calling me—I can almost hear it. He is just beyond this bridge. My throat goes dry.

I step onto the bridge, leaving a boot print in the gathering snow.

The woman's singing, deep and low, cuts into my heart with her longing.

I repeat the words. "A land…from a lullaby?" Yes, if the man lives anywhere, it would be in such a place.

I see the word blue in my head. The same shade as his eyes.

I reach the summit and hold my breath. Is it wrong to try and find him? I find, I don't care.

I leap over the apex.

Chapter 8

Next Evening

"Are you all right, True?" Ram turned, placing the final dinner dish in the cupboard.

David, one of the teens, interjected, "You're so white. Dude, you're always pale, but tonight you're freakin' *pasty.*"

"Brilliant, thanks." Truman rolled his eyes.

Dave shrugged, walking out of the kitchen.

Truman massaged his face with both hands, his fingers stopping in a steepled prayer position before his lips.

He stared at Ram. "Dunno. I think it's the new one we're expecting. Don't know if I'm up to it. I mean, Todd, and his tantrums, David and Ethan with their fabulous adolescence, oppositional defiance disorder and detachment. Maybe I should've said no."

"Well, your *problem* doesn't help the situation, does it?"

"*Which* problem? Don't start on me, Ram. I'm in no mood. I've been pricked, prodded and wired up to more machines than should be humanly permissible."

"It's emotion-color synesthesia, it has a name and we should use it. It isn't some sort of weird, new-agey ability." His hands fluttered and he pulled a face. "It's a cross-wiring of your senses—we've been over this."

Truman hesitated. *Should I tell him everything?* It would mean another endless round of battles, with Ram insisting on more tests.

I need to prove to myself I'm not mental.

"There's something I've never told you."

Ram's eyebrows traveled up his forehead into his jet-black hair. "I knew it! I knew you were holding out on me! Your P.E.T. scans were the most original I'd ever seen. Spill it. I cannot be-*lieve* you didn't tell me everything." His expression changed from surprise to irritation in a tick.

"I'm sorry. Look, I already feel like a freak, you know? It's what kept me from being adopted till I was what, fourteen? Because I opened my big, fat mouth and was labeled abnormal. So, forgive me if I'm not the most trusting sort when it comes to psychologists."

"You're stalling." His foot tapped. "And I'm your best friend."

"Fine." He stood up and paced back and forth in front of the kitchen sink. "I can also…*feel* people, for who they are…their personalities, their singularity, if you will."

Ram's face re-lit with the familiar scientific fascination he'd come to despise. "Go on, man. How?"

"Again, it's subjective, naturally, to how I assess them, I suppose—but typically it's spot on."

Ram stood and pulled open a drawer, scrabbling around till he extracted a notebook and pen. He clicked the pen up. "Give me an example."

Anger simmered. Truman bit his bottom lip. He struggled not to bite his analytical head off.

He opted to scratch one eyebrow, and roll his eyes. Ram was compulsively curious.

"Like you, I've told you, your color is brown. But what I didn't tell you, was the sensations which go with brown. I smell chocolate, and feel...compassion, when you're around."

Ram laughed out loud.

"Look, I know how it sounds—*shut-it*, or I'll quit."

He wiped the smile from his face, and motioned to continue, pen poised. He was doing his psychologist shtick.

Truman bit back a growl. "Ok." He took a huge breath, and blurted, "The girl from the other night, in the corn."

"The one we aren't certain is real? The one I am fully convinced was a dream, created by your self-imposed abstinence? Perhaps resulting in a testosterone-fueled psychotic break?"

"Quit joking!"

"Who's joking?"

"Yes, well that *dream*-girl was a strangely beautiful shade of lavender, one I've never seen before. And she felt…" His cheeks went hot.

Ram's mouth dropped. "I'm astounded. Mr. I-have-no-interest-in-women-they-are-all-shallow-and-beneath-me just blushed."

Truman squeezed his eyes shut. He didn't want to watch his reaction. "I felt her pain and fear like a black tsunami, dousing me." His hands mimed the positions. "And below it, submerged, was a crystal pure feeling, the same I get with ice or snowflakes. Purity, maybe?"

He was surprised to hear footsteps. He opened his eyes. Now Ram was the one pacing.

"We have to tell Dr. Kinney at the lab. You have

sets of synesthesia going on in there." He tapped the side of his head.

Guilt plagued him, for editing. His mind also calculated facial expressions-analyzing them into complex patterns. The human lie detector. Ram would *never* let him be if he confessed it.

I am so not talking about the journal. He'll have me committed.

"No. I'm done with all the testing. It's going nowhere."

"Don't be stupid, what if your gift could help others?"

"Gift? That's stretching it a bit. If you fire me, I could get a job as a carny, though. Come one, come all—see the human name-taster!"

Images filled his head. He stood alongside the president or prime minister, as they simultaneously requested he assess the personality or intentions of a foreigner standing before them. Or if they were lying. *No, thanks.*

"I'm going out."

He flung open the back door, leaving Ram with his mouth gaping again.

He jogged toward the corn. Entering the rows, the familiar color cut the air, and he felt her presence. His heart swelled, screaming at him to find her. He barreled to the bridge.

His mind sped, flight of ideas really. He'd read about *Soul Mates*—their mythological origins. He thought it all bollocks.

But what if the perfect person for you, happened to be born in the wrong century? What then?

"Then this bloody cornfield."

It made sense, in a fair, but twisted sort of way.

Somewhere to his left, music began. Music?

His heart jack-hammered.

Oh, no, oh, no. I am losing it.

He stopped dead as recognition struck. The music crackled, like his father's antique Victrola.

"I don't believe it."

Judy Garland was singing. *Somewhere over the Rainbow.*

If any song encapsulated his childhood, his fears—this was it. He'd first heard it at the orphanage, fell in love with her, wanted to step into her world, at the age of six.

It was the one part of the song. He couldn't believe it when he'd heard it. It was if God was answering his prayers, that he wasn't a freak, wasn't alone with his oddity.

If a place existed, *where trouble smelled like lemon drops*, then surely, that was the place for him.

He laughed out loud.

A few years older and wiser, he learned they *melted*, not *smelled.*

He bolted again, Judy's voice sound-tracking his experience like some 1940's film. Following him toward the bridge.

Toward her, the nameless girl, he'd felt love, overprotection…but now desire wolfed down the other sentiments, consuming him.

Somewhere along the way, he'd cut his neck. He swiped it away.

The rustling corn, the thunder, the crickets, all faded to nothing. He was consumed with a singular thought.

The woman in white. My reader. *What is your name?*

* * *

My boots slide in the snow, gathering on the bridge. Anything, anywhere, must be better than Salem. The sound of the hornets in my head whir in protest. *They don't like freedom, they thrive on pain.*

I hurtle myself to the top, directly at the bridge's apex.

I connect, with a hard-cold-wall of blackness. Sparks conjure out of nothing, exploding from my impact. Multi-colored and beautiful, they fizzle immediately, suffocated by snowflakes.

My head snaps back, shooting pain down my spine. I sprawl in a heap, sliding backwards on the slick boards. My head darts up, I'm riveted. And angry.

It's like a wall.

The air churns in a rectangle, and whispers come and go. It's as if the world is cut in two. Snow gathers around my feet, falling in huge white clusters. But only two steps more, on his side, the corn is green, lush and full.

I hear footsteps beating up the other side. My heart stutters, knowing *it's him.*

I stand, and rush to the door, placing my hands against it, unsure if he can see me.

Little zaps of light envelope my hands, twisting down my fingers up to my arms.

I can't move. I'm not afraid. I can't move.

He bursts into the clearing. My stomach bottoms,

and a hot, driving urge rushes through my veins. It is him. My writer and the man from the other day, they are indeed, one and the same.

He pauses for but a moment, his face auditioning a cast of emotions; surprise, concern, yearning, and finally joy.

He bolts up the other side, yelling, "Are you all right? Come closer, I—"

He collides with the door, hands spread like mine. Our hands overlap, but don't touch. The door separates us.

The rainbow colored lightning overtakes his hands, melding him to the other side.

I am panting like an animal. His face is so close, I could taste his breath, if not for the wretched door.

His blue-green eyes widen before I feel it, but then a shock vibrates me, hard enough to rattle my teeth. His eyes are fearful, I know for me.

His mouth moves, but no words come out.

Then I see it, in my mind. The cornfield disappears.

I see him, as a baby, and his crying mother. She slips him into a woman's outstretched arms, and flees the room, sobbing. She flies past a sign that reads, Applegate Orphanage.

A swirl of light and pain.

He's a boy now. I shudder. I feel his hunger, as acutely as if it's my own. And his loneliness. It crushes me, and my lips part—I can't cry out. He swings alone in a dirty play yard.

More pain, a sensation of falling.

I see him again, he's almost his age now, just a

little younger. Sitting at a desk, staring at a book with a million letters and numbers that mean nothing to me. I feel the loneliness, though. It feels exactly as it did when he was a boy. Only now, it's mixed with anger.

He grabs a container before him, spilling a bunch of small pills into his hand. He glares at them. His hand shakes, sending some flying onto the desk. Seething hatred fills him, fills me, and he pelts them against the wall. I hear their tapping as they rain down to the floor.

I'm back with him now. His eyes are contracting, and widening, not really seeing me. His mouth twitches, and his lips are moving—but I hear nothing. My hands begin to warm by bits, like ice dethawing, and suddenly I can feel his rough hands.

I am alive, for the first time.

* * *

He feels her presence. The wind is whipping crazy, and Ram will undoubtedly call the psych ward.

"I can't go back. Not yet. And now I'm talking to myself."

He laughed, but it died in his mouth as he broke through the corn.

There she was, standing frozen on the center of the bridge, her hands held up on either side of her as if under arrest.

Her red hair whips around her, and her expression is terrified. She shudders, the rest of her body moving while her hands remain seemingly glued to thin air.

He charges toward her, covering the ground in

seconds.

"Are you all right? Come closer, I—"

His hands fuse to the invisible door. A charge like lightning gyrates his arms, legs.

What's happening?

Her eyes stare, boring into him with their beautiful intensity. Her lips, parted and full, an inch away. He licks his lips, a scream building in his chest.

And then his mind fills. Expanding, bursting—with her memories.

She's a wee thing, with her family. The sound of shrieks and drumbeats fill the air. Villagers flee from all around.

Her father hauls a little boy over his shoulders, and grasps her hand, vaulting her into a cabin. He throws her mother a gun. The boy is wailing behind her legs.

He feels her fear, bordering on insanity. The Micmaq burst through the door. A tomahawk flies, burying itself in her father's chest. He falls to one knee.

The Indian wrenches his hair with one hand, and with the other, scalps the tomahawk across his skull. Skinning him like a hunter skins a rabbit.

The girl, her, drops to the ground, and the boy scrambles around her neck like a frightened animal. His wailing doesn't stop.

Her mother is wrenched from her side, and she wails as loud as the boy.

A shudder, another volt.

She stands in the center of a circle. Grown now. A circle of girl's chant. 'Say goodbye to one eye, say goodbye to one eye.'

One throws an apple, aimed at her mismatched eyes.

And then a barrage of rotted fruits whiz by as she ducks. She darts, back and forth, trying to escape the circle.

A jab to the chest, and he can see her face again.

She is utterly beautiful. His breath catches. He feels his hands warming. And can suddenly feel her skin.

I can feel her skin.

The door whirls, and pops, and disappears.

Our heads clank together.

* * *

His lips finally find mine. I feel his hands around my waist, gripping me tightly. I breathe in, and I feel so alive, my blood rushing to every piece of me. Waking me from a terrible sleep.

"Are you all right? Oh bloody—look what I've done to your lip!"

And he stares down at me. His blue-green, almond shaped eyes scrutinize the lump rising on my cheek. He winces, forehead wrinkling under dark, untidy hair.

"Can you talk?" His fingers brush away the trickle of blood from the side of my mouth. His face is unsure. "Did you, see anything, while we were stuck there?"

His touch is exceedingly gentle, like the brush of a feather. I shiver, and an unfamiliar longing roars at my core. I am forgetting to speak, gaping at him like an idiot.

"I-I'm intact. In pain, but I will survive. And yes, I saw many things."

"Me, too."

His thin lips break into a relieved grin, turned up on one side. It takes my breath away. I haven't seen such a carefree smile since I was a child.

He sobers quickly, his eyes roving over me as if checking for more injuries.

"I'm so glad yer all right. And so glad yer *real.* I'm not mental after all."

The brow wrinkles again. His right eye is swelling from the impact. I stand on tip-toes, my lips almost touching it before I clench my teeth, and pull back.

He stands back, examining my clothes. "Do you work at a history-comes-alive place?" His right eyebrow rises in question. The smell of him is over powering. *Cleaner* than any man I'd ever been near, yet decidedly masculine. I swallow again, fighting my completely irrational urges. My mind races a streak of impossible thoughts, leaving me feeling like a common strumpet.

"What is *that*?" His lips purse in concern, as he gazes up at two moons. His expression changes, to something that looks like acceptance. "Those are the clothes you wear every day, aren't they?"

Shame reddens my face. I absently stroke my dress. "Yes, I am a servant now. I was once a gentleman's daughter, but that seems another life ago."

Comprehension dawns on his face—that he's embarrassed me. He quickly takes my hand, to stop its fidgeting.

He steps toward me, boldly returning his arms to

my waist. “That wasn’t what I meant. I am so pleased you’re here. That doesn’t matter to me. Do you remember seeing me before? That night in the corn?”

“Of course.” My face flushes again. *I must be bold.*

This may be like a fae tale, and no doubt, my time with him will be limited. Like everything good I’ve ever known. “I’ve thought of nothing else for weeks. Since I found your journal.”

His eyes widen. “I-I’m honored.” His eyes drop. “I cannot get you out of my head. It’s been every day, every minute.” They flick back up and his expression narrows. “And I know that sounds completely mental—but here...” his eyes scan the stalks and he shivers, “This may be where crazy and reality meet. I feel I already know you—like I always have.” I feel his chest still, holding his breath, awaiting my response.

“As do I.” I search my feelings, to see if it rings true. *It does.* Being in his arms is like a homecoming. My mind screams at me to *be sensible*.

But this unfamiliar longing, this *need*, will not be silent.

It’s *more* than wanting to kiss him. His eyes see me. Each moment of his attention restores me; like the ghost of my soul is returning, becoming flesh and blood once again.

He was the draw in the corn. The empty sighing inside me is silenced, and the hornets are nowhere to be found. I smile maliciously. *Good.*

“Good sir, I know this to be highly improper, but I must speak.”

“First, tell me your name?”

"Verity Montague. And yours?"

"Truman Johnstone."

"Verity, please excuse my *forwardness*." He shifts me slightly in his arms, but to my relief, makes no sign of releasing me. "Wot year is it?"

"1692. Good sir Johnstone, why would you ask me such?"

"Please, just call me True. Because, Verity," his eyes stare up at the sky, flicking right and left, "I see two moons, and I don't see *how* that's possible. Here, where you stand, it is the twenty-first century."

My mouth drops open, my limbs turn to stone. The inside of my mind does a revolution, and I struggle not to swoon.

"What sort of enchantment be this?" I push away from his chest. Fear is returning.

Is he a warlock, sent to entice me, seduce me? The book, the book, I wrote in the book.

So the townsfolk can finally convict me?

I stare at him.

"They are about to accuse me of witchcraft, perhaps they are right? Am I responsible for my arrival in this unnatural place, in my fervent desire to see you again? Oh, God, please forgive me." My legs go to water and buckle, my knees scraping the hard ground.

Fear smites my gut and resurges with a new intensity, punishing me for a few stolen moments of happiness, the swarm buzzes in my mind.

He drops beside me; his eyes are tight and careful. His hands slide around the small of my back again. He cradles me like a child and I inhale his scent; tears well at this tenderness.

No one has held me, save John, since my

childhood disappeared.

His muscles tense under my hands.

His voice hums through his throat as he speaks into my ear. “I refuse to believe this strange power you have over me is witchcraft. I think it’s a gift. I can’t imagine someone’s name that feels and tastes so pure, could be wicked?”

I pull back to stare. My tethered self-control is unraveling again, and with trembling fingers, I touch his lips.

I should not. I should not.

A smoldering instinct blazes to life, incinerating my concern. My head dips forward. My lips are so close, they brush his.

He whispers fervently, “You aren’t responsible for this, and if you say you’re not a witch-you are not. I think this place, the corn, is...an anomaly. Something I’m a bit of an expert on, seeing as I am one.”

“What is an…anomaly?” I try to focus, but he’s so close, I cannot concentrate.

“I think this place somehow yoked our time periods. I haven’t the slightest idea how. I always hated physics.”

His expression wanes, and he’s breathing harder, as if he’s only realized how close I am to him.

His blue eyes widen, and his words spill out. I listen intently, trying to catch them all.

“I needed to see you again. And here you are. I’ve dreamt of you every night, since the first night. I am going to speak plainly, because I don’t know if this place will last, or fade off into the night like a bloody Brigadoon.”

I open my mouth to ask whatever a Brigadoon is,

but he cuts across me.

"Tell me *why* you are in pain. You were crying?"

I sigh, and drop my head, fiddling with a bit of lace on my dress. It's as if Salem's fear seeps across the bridge, a poisonous fog, leeching into my brain to ruin this precious moment.

"I know not what will become of me, Truman. I told you my parents were killed in the Indian raids and I am now a maidservant, with a younger brother under my care. A brother who is…different. I am different, though I hide it." I pause, ever careful with the subject. But the words tumble out. "There are more men than women in Salem—"

"Salem, Massachusetts? What year did you say it was?" His eyes crinkle. "I cannot believe I just said that."

"And without fortune or a family to recommend me, I'm not a fit bride for any, save John Holcomb, whom I detest. He's a drunk and a lazy—"

"Verity, someone called you a witch? Who did?"

"Many. Most recently Constable Corwin, who insists my presence, be a prelude to the fits. It is a terrible thing, Truman. Everyone in town is accused or afflicted. It's as if Satan himself has taken up residence."

His gaze intensifies and he chews his bottom lip.

I admit, "I'm frightened."

I feel his hand shake and realize it's because he is holding mine. Suddenly, his expression is as terrified as I feel.

His eyes are squinting, serious. "Verity, stay here. Stay with me." His voice is thick and hoarse, and he swallows to clear it. His prominent Adam's apple bobs with the effort. "You are not safe. I'll help you."

"I-I can't, even if I wanted to. My brother, he is still there. He needs me—to help him. He does not understand people, nor they-him. *They hate him.* He has no one, save me."

"Just stay, for now. I can still make out your moon on the other side, so the door's open. Tell me about you. I have so many questions. Tell me about a time when you were happy?"

I hesitate for a moment, feeling the pull of responsibility. It beckons over the bridge and time, but the feel of his thumb, stroking the back of my hand is like a song.

Only time will tell, if it be a hymn or a siren-song.

He holds my hand and pulls me to sit. His serious eyes never leave mine.

The music restarts in the corn. Not scary now, more like one of my mother's lullabies.

His eyes widen a moment, then he recovers. I *must* know if he is like me…*odd.* "Do you hear it, then?"

Both eyebrows rise in surprise. "*Yes*. I don't think anyone else I live with hears the music. It isn't frightening tonight, though. It's rather soothing, isn't it?"

I feel foolish, but ask anyway. "Is *this* the land of lullabies?"

Truman's whole face seems to twitch, then he laughs. "Erm, no. But I've heard that song here, too."

He tugs me closer to him, and my body folds into him without permission.

I talk for hours, my secrets falling out of my lips like I'm confessing my sins.

He tells me about how he is different, too.

Filling in the holes from the pages and visions I've seen. How he never knew love of any kind, till fourteen.

He wipes every tear that leaks down my cheeks. And I feel a reluctant thrill with every touch.

I finish, unable to admit another word, or painful memory. I face him.

His eyes smolder, and he's holding his breath. I slide closer, resting my forehead against his. His heartbeat quickens under my hand. His breath rushes out.

His eyelids half-close, and his rough fingers leave little scorching streaks where they trace my cheekbones. My heart beat accelerates, like a bullet fired, matching his. I am not going to be able to stop. My guilt and my longing battle—my mind against my fragile heart.

"I am afraid I'll never see you again," he whispers. "I've never connected with any girl. It was like I was a soldier trying to talk to socialites. We had nothing in common."

"I—" I try to stop his words, pulverizing my heart.

His soft lips crush mine, and I feel his tongue, hot in my mouth. My whole body convulses. His hands slide round, hoisting me onto his lap.

Fear and duty and the stocks nag my conscience. I should push him away, but I do not. I cannot.

There is a bonding, it feels almost holy.

He pulls back to regard me. "I want you to stay. There has to be a way…"

I have no answer. *I* silence *him* this time. My lips

part his, and I bite his bottom lip.

I've never kissed anyone this way before.

The situation is impossible. I beat back the pain, crouching around my heart, waiting for my return. It is inexcusable to give into despair with him so close. I refuse to waste the feeling of him under me.

I take a deep breath, but cowardly close my eyes. "Make me feel *completely* alive, before I die again, when I step back across that bridge."

He makes a quiet noise, kissing me harder.

I can almost touch the bonding, feeling it flow and ebb between us. A living, pulsing, captured lightning, intertwining our bodies.

As his hands race up and down my back, I finally understand why the other girls are so obsessed with men, and marriage. I'd choose to stay here, if I could.

To even live in this dangling spot of time.

His lips leave my mouth and trail down my neck. His calloused fingers trace along my collarbone with such tenderness, tears spring in my eyes. I remember the lashings, the stocks, the sting in my cheek after the blows.

It seems he is trying to commit every inch of me to memory. *Pain crushes my insides. How will I bare these memories, when I am alone again?*

A gale picks up, blowing a flurry of leaves against us. The stalks writhe, undulating like underwater reeds in a current.

The passion drains from his face, and he hauls me to stand. "I think the door to Salem is closing, your moon is gone."

"I must get back!"

His eyes are a deep well of pain, but he dusts off

my dress.

"Please, keep checking the door. I will too. This cannot be all there is…" His voice rises with a fierce anger. I cringe involuntarily. My mouth spasms, but I can't respond.

His grip tightens as we dart headlong toward the bridge. Our footsteps echo as the old wood creaks under us. We reach the top.

"I don't think I can go further," he says, reaching the top of the arch. "This is where you disappeared last time."

I stare at him, indecision tearing my heart like a wishbone. I can never leave John, but I long to remain with Truman, to hear his words, to touch him….

"Come with *me*, Truman."

His face is agony. His lips open, and he bites the lower one. "I-I so want to." His face turns to look at the house, visible over the corn tops.

His grip crushes my shoulders, and he folds me into him. "I've never wanted anything more," his hoarse voice whispers into my ear.

He places a final rough kiss on my mouth. He pushes me back. His eyes are glistening.

The wind picks up, swirling my hair into my face. Below my boots, the bridge rumbles up and down like a thunderclap has overtaken it, infusing it with life. Warning me.

"Please don't forget me." My eyes flick away. The pain is waiting. It lurks at the bottom of the bridge.

"That isn't physically possible. You never leave my head." His voice is fierce.

I clutch at my throat, ripping off my necklace. My

only memento of my mother. The little heart is so important to me—I irrationally feel this gesture must *somehow* bind us together-no matter the time.

"So you shan't forget me."

"I don't want you to go, Verity. I'd do anything to change it. I don't know how. Be careful. Please come back—*tomorrow*—if the door is open. Surely, it will open."

I step out of his embrace and across the flexuous line in space, dividing the bridge in two. "I will, Truman."

I feel the warmth of his fingers slip as I take the final crucial step.

And.

I am alone on the bridge. Falling clusters of snowflakes gather in my hair, immediately dowsing my dress. The taste of him lingers in my mouth.

Turning back to the spot where he had stood, I reach my hand up to feel the fluid-air, but all that remains is a gust of wind.

He is gone.

Chapter 9

The morning sun shone through Truman's window, heating one side of his face till it itched. He squinted at the laptop screen, and trying futilely to rub the sting out of his eyes. The words were blurring. He hadn't slept since he left Verity in the corn.

How could he? His mind played devil's advocate, telling him she was a stress-induced hallucination; but his body wouldn't hear of it.

He sniffed his sleeve...then inhaled deeply; her scent still clung to his clothing. His mind couldn't leave her, returning again and again to her skin, her face. His fingers absently rubbed together. He could almost feel her spiral curls around his fingers.

He reached inside his trouser pocket, pulling out her delicate silver locket. His tangible proof she existed. He smiled. Should he hide it? *If Ram found it*…he wasn't ready to tell him.

The locket shone in the sunlight, sending a shower of reflective sparkles glittering on the wall.

He decided, a little sheepishly, to wear it.

She was real, so he wasn't crazy. But she'd sparked a new kind of madness.

His mind, chock-full of layered images, analyzed her every gesture, every pull of her mouth. It felt bloated, ready to burst.

How would he think of anything else? Everything else paled against his desire to see her again.

A strange, gnawing fear was growing. It said, '*you won't see her again.*' As if one afternoon of pure happiness was his life's quota.

His thick fingers fumbled with the locket's tiny clasp, but he finally managed to get it around his neck. He slipped it under his sweater. He was smitten, but not an idiot.

His lips twitched, and he smiled. Keeping perspective had never been a problem before, but it was definitely a problem now.

Ram would take the Mickey out of him for this totally whipped gesture.

He will not believe me.

"I don't care." The sound of his voice in the morning silence was jarring. His heart ping-ponged between exultation and apprehension.

"I just should've went with her."

But guilt at even the thought of that selfishness swatted down the mental volley.

He closed his eyes, took a deep breath and squared his shoulders. The feel of the tiny heart against his chest gave him something tangible, a reminder she was real, *somewhere*.

Something shimmered on his bicep. Another living testament that she wasn't fiction. A singular, red strand glittered with golden highlights in the sun.

He left it there. Staring at it.

You are acting like a school-boy.

He smiled so wide his face hurt.

He balanced the laptop precariously on his bed,

hitting the Google search for the third straight hour.

He typed, '*Salem Witch Trials Verity Montague*' again.

"You have to be somewhere, Verity."

No results found, glared back from the screen.

No such person appeared to have been associated with the trials.

He scrolled through now familiar names, searching for anything. Some distant relative?

Mercy Lewis, Reverend Parris, Tituba…and finally, the words, *Maine Indian Raids*.

"Yes!" he whooped, and then quickly covered his mouth, checking the time.

Five a.m.

Only a half hour remained till the morning pandemonium. The high school portion of the orphans would wake within the hour. As if on cue, a shuffling pair of sock-clad feet past his door, enroute to the bathroom.

His eyes flicked back to the screen, reading furiously.

The Maine Indian Raids left young Mercy Lewis orphaned, so Reverend George Burroughs took her in; they eventually moved south to Salem, Mass. Ultimately, Mercy ended up as a servant in the Putnam household, where she too, became afflicted. Mercy was supposedly visited by many of her fellow parishioners in spectral form. All it took was an accusatory proclamation by one of the afflicted girls for the authorities to bring in the defendant for questioning. So, if one was unpopular, such as Sarah Good, who was many times widowed, and had to resort to begging...

He scanned further down.

Or if one was deemed different, in a Puritan time so set upon sameness, these ones were optimal targets for accusation, and subsequent hanging. Indeed, the Puritans were a superstitious lot, mistrusting peoples with red hair—anything unfamiliar was to be considered as a possible witch.

An impossible hole ripped open his chest, accompanied by a sensation of falling. He fell into fear's gaping mouth, its gnashing circle quickly morphing into the hangman's noose.

"Oh, Verity. Why aren't you mentioned here? Where are you in history?"

His eyes shot around the room, unseeing; looking futilely for answers.

His eyebrow rose.

A wooden box, another gift from his father, was cracked open a fraction of an inch.

Irritation rose with his brows. The children were not allowed in his room, let alone in his personal effects.

He leapt off the bed, heading over to it.

Cracking it open, he paused, staring at the contents.

What? Who?

The box was brimming with canary-yellow candies. At least they *looked* like candy?

He plucked one out, and popped it in his mouth.

Lemon drops?

He lifted a handful, sliding them into his pocket.

At the bottom, slipped under the candy, was a yellowing, ancient piece of paper.

His heart skittered and stutter-stepped against his ribcage.

He carefully slid the candies off, unfolding it. Bits of parchment sprinkled down to the floor.

~ ~ ~

Where fears are born, and given legs,
A place to grieve, to heal, to beg.
To dare to dream, to face your fear,
And rescue what you hold most dear.

~ ~ ~

Ice water trickled through his veins, solidifying in his legs, which now felt heavy and weak. Again the surreal feeling. He half-wondered if Dave had a camera planted in his room somewhere.

Ram poked his head in the door.

He jumped two feet. "Fer the love of all that's holy, do you ever bloody knock?"

His hand dropped guiltily, trying nonchalantly to hide the paper behind his back.

Ram's eyes were wary. "You coming down or what? Breakfast won't make itself, you know. Plus, they're bringing the new boy for O.T., then he's to stay."

"Yes, well I'm sure that O.T. session will make him incredibly happy. He'll be thinking from the frying pan to the fire." He laughed. It sounded bitter. "I think the bureaucrats who write the rules for therapy should have to actually implement them one day."

"Isn't that what you had on yesterday?"

Ram's dark eyes narrowed, but a boy's call distracted him and he left, padding down the hall. His face said he wasn't awake enough for interrogation.

Hesitating, he plucked Verity's hair from his arm, and folded it into the locket. He snapped it shut, giving the laptop one last look. He stared at the parchment, deciding.

He placed it back under the lemon drops. If he carried it on him, it would disintegrate by day's end.

He'd already memorized it, anyway. He wondered who had written it. And if he really wanted to know.

He followed Ram down the stairs, nodding when expected at his conversation, but inside, the words from the internet kept repeating, 'they were hanged for being different'.

* * *

I cling to Mercy's arm. We huddle together in the back seat of the carriage as it rattles into Salem Town.

A storm rages on, as it has for days, fueling the tempers of the men in the carriage. Thomas Putnam, his brother Edward, Joseph Hutchinson and Thomas Preston argue all the way, each with his own particular opinion about the fate of the accused.

Mercy and I trail behind the men as we file into the building. Awaiting our troop is a somber-faced John Corwin. And to his right, an equally distressed John Hathorne.

"It's the hanging judge," I whisper, low enough so only Mercy can hear.

"Constables," begins Thomas Putnam, "it grieves us greatly to convene, but action must be taken."

I feel Mercy tighten beneath my hand; an undulation of muscles courses up her arm like an invisible vice. Mercy's eyes turn to me, wide with horror as the fit arrives.

Her expression is a woman falling.

"Good Sir Putnam, she be afflicted again!" I scream.

Mercy collapses in a heap, her head hammering on the wood floor like Indian war-drums. The sound unearths long-buried visions.

Dead, scalped bodies. The sweet smell of burning flesh.

Sweat beads my brow and the hornets restart their song.

Mercy's limp hand reaches up as her eyes roll white in her head. She manages a strangled, wet cry.

"Oh Mercy, oh Mercy."

I drop beside her, cradling her hand, letting my touch tell her I will protect her. *If I can.*

The shaking stops. Mercy's pink tongue juts out between her parted lips.

I give it a discrete poke, tucking it back in her cheek.

I gather her into my arms and rock; just as I've rocked John through so many nights of pain.

"Give her to me, Verity."

Thomas Putnam stoops, sweeping Mercy into his arms. He ferries her into a back room, following the direction of Constable Corwin's outstretched finger.

I hurry behind, hovering, waiting.

After a long whispered conversation, they finally leave us. I perch beside Mercy on the rickety cot. The door is ajar, and their voices filter in through the darkness.

"As you can see, the fits seem to be stronger than an epilepsy. Much mischief has been done to Elizabeth Parris, Abigail Williams, Ann Putnam and Elizabeth Hubbard. Sundry times, within these two months, and lately also done at Salem Village contrary to the peace of our Sovereign Lord and Lady William and Mary, King and Queen of England…."*

Their voices are drowned by the scream of hornets infesting my ears.

I cup my hands over them, but it's no use.

I see the word hornets, dripped in purple flames, and picture them licking along my ear canal on their way to eat my addled brain.

My mind flips through the pictures of the accused like a horrid walk to the gallows. Bridget Bishop. Tituba. John.

All different. None meant any harm nor malice. My hands shake again.

Hathorne's voice cuts through my terror-fog, silencing my hateful insects. "I hereby issue warrants for Sarah Good, Tituba Indian, and Sarah Osborne under suspicion of witchcraft."

**Starred portions are snippets from the original transcripts of this meeting.*

Chapter 10

Truman squared his shoulders and inhaled deeply, preparing his mind. Each hour in Occupational Therapy was a physical, mental cage-match.

April, the social worker from their sister orphanage, dragged the slip of a girl down the entrance hall, into the clinic. Her tiny body flopped to the floor, flailing against April's hand, which encircled her wrist. The woman's tall frame tottered on her high heels. She looked like a flamingo, tilting on one leg as the writhing girl knocked her off balance.

Truman vaulted to the rescue, taking the little girl's hand in his own.

Tiny, tearful eyes met his as she howled in disdain. Her eyes darted like a trapped animal, taking in the unfamiliar surroundings.

"So the orders are a continuous feeding at night by the tube and she is now P.O. during the day?"

He automatically lifted his foot, blocking a kick from her tiny tennis shoe without glancing down.

"What's P.O.?" April looked harried.

Her normally perfect hair hung in her face. She examined her manicure for injuries. Truman fought the urge to roll his eyes.

"I mean she is allowed to eat, now? Her barium

swallow came back without precautions? Her file said she was aspirating on thin liquids before, leaking into her lungs—the cause of the frequent pneumonia?"

"Yes, yes. I hope you fare better than us. She's eaten nothing since we took her in a day ago. If it continues, we'll have to take her in for dehydration."

Truman took a mental sigh. "We're okay. You're a distraction. I'll have Sunshine text you when we're through."

April's face was decidedly relieved as she closed the door to the clinic.

Even professionals don't know what to do with these kids, his mind retorted to her expression.

He released the girl. She backed away, never taking her eyes off him. Black, wild hair flowed from her head, reaching her buttocks. It was *woolly* with thick tangles and knots.

She was like a little black sheep; welcome to my world, little one. The smile splitting his lips was painful. And familiar.

Sunshine entered, closing the door. The girl bolted forward, intent on escape. The door slammed a second before she could slip her foot out. Her body collapsed to the floor; she flailed, kicking and spitting.

Her tiny chin quivered. A wail, shrill as nails on a chalkboard, ripped from her mouth.

She flipped over, swinging like mad. Her forehead smashed against the floor with a wet thud.

"Oh, come on."

Truman flew for her, but Sunshine arrived first, pulling the child into her arms.

She hummed a lullaby in her ear.

"Oh, Truman." She kept her eyes downcast.

She bit her lip, wrestling to keep her professional face on; but her voice had a telling quake.

The girl was getting under his assistant's skin.

She was outlined in black—the color he associated with physical pain.

Sunshine's color was red; a direct contradiction to her typical resplendent shade of orange. It now flickered like dappled sunlight as her feelings shifted.

Her dark hair fell in a curtain, hiding her expression.

Truman summoned his emotional wall. "She's been neglected, I'm guessing since day one. The file says her father was an alcoholic and in jail, and her mother was declared mentally incompetent to stand trial. That hair hasn't had a brush run through it in years. We might have to shave it."

He fought the mental slideshow threatening behind his barricade.

His six-year-old self; filthy, smelly. Crying.

No, get it together. That was then. Make a difference now.

He kneeled, squirting warm lotion onto his hands and rubbing them together.

Carefully, he peeled off a tiny sock, leaving a ring of dirt lingering around her ankle.

She smelled like a rest-stop urinal.

He moved his hands in practiced, deep circles of massage and the girl instantly stilled, entranced.

"Wow, that's working," Sunshine whispered. "What a difference from Timmy."

Truman raised a skeptical eyebrow. "Too early for that assumption, Watson."

He grasped a tiny hand, and began to rub.

A primal scream erupted; she twisted, recoiling as if a million needles lodged under her fingernails.

She lunged backwards in a head-butt. Sunshine juked out of the way.

"You spoke too soon," Truman said, still rubbing. "She's tactilely defensive. Her nerves are working overtime. Think Princess and the Pea, but all over. Particularly with her hands."

Sunshine released her and walked across the clinic, searching desperately for a toy. Anything to distract her.

Wild, dark eyes screamed at him. She lunged, shrieking in his face.

He met her gaze, holding very still. He shifted to the other hand, intensifying the massaging motions.

"If she can't stand to touch things, she won't eat either."

The girl gagged at the word *eat*, filling his lap with a white, chunky, pile of sick.

He sighed. "Sunny, a little help here?"

* * *

Disgust burns my nose. Only hours have passed since Mercy's fit, yet here she sits, prim and judgmental; encouraging Anne Jr. to condemn another in this endless night that's conquered Salem.

"Who was it, Anne?" Mercy prods. "Was it Goody Proctor or Goody Osborne?"

"Yes, tell us child, whose spectral form torments you? Be it Sarah Good?" Anne Sr. prompts.

I peek around the corner to see Anne Jr. on the chair by the fire, her gaze unfocused.

"Someone sits in Grandmother's chair across from me, even now. She is pale."

I pretend to sweep near the main room, needing to hear Anne, Jr.'s condemnations.

I do not trust that girl. At times, she does appear afflicted, but others—I think she craves the attention. Needs it like a drunkard to his drink.

"Be it one of the Parris family?

I step into the other room, suppressing my gasp.

John's stare is quizzical.

"What? What is going on?"

John is unable to decipher emotions. In order for him to understand someone's anger, the person need strike him or curse him to his face.

The *language* of the eyes, that's oft in complete contradiction to people's words, is foreign to him. I am his interpreter.

My brother isn't stupid, quite the opposite, but his inability to decipher faces left him constantly guessing, and anxious.

I sigh, wishing that the intensity of my love for him, would heal him. He feels like an immigrant, even among his own people.

"Goodwife Putnam just suggested *another*! I know not what shall become of this town."

"Aye, Goody Nurse was always kind to me. Look what happened to her."

"No, it could not be?"

"Pray what, sister? Speak plainly."

"The Putnams have argued with the Nurses as long as I can recall about where their land halts, and the Nurses' begins. Do you suppose they would suggest this to Anne to influence her? To get the land?"

John shrugs. "Some people's hearts are black as ink."

I grin. No doubt John took considerable time working out that comparison. And practiced it.

Anne Jr.'s voice rings out, and we both turn toward the sitting area. "Yes, I do believe it *was* Goodwife Nurse, ma'am."

My mouth pops open, along with the floodgate of fear.

"As I live and breathe, John. Goodwife Nurse's breaths be numbered. No soul be safe in Salem."

Chapter 11

Saturday, October 28th, 5:30 a.m.

Dawn was seeping through the clouds again, its filtered rays shining through a mostly overcast morning.

Truman hurriedly typed '*Salem Witch Trials*' into the search engine and held his breath.

A tottering pile of books surrounded him, all on the subject at hand. He stifled a yawn.

Obsession was Ram's diagnosis. His fingers compulsively rubbed Verity's locket. His eyes flicked to the calendar.

Two weeks. No letters. No contact. No moon. Nothing.

If not for the bit of silver between his fingers, he'd be doubting his own sanity by now.

Sweat dampened his palms. He opened the journal to the last entry, re-reading it for the fifteenth time.

~ ~ ~

Truman...the whole town seems enchanted. People are accusing John. It's only a matter of time 'til they come for me. I will keep checking the door. I so wish to see you again. I fear I am not long for this world.

~ ~ ~

It'd been too long since he saw her. Each day, a worried, aching need burrowed deeper into his heart like an emotive parasite.

Only one thing would halt it: to see her, touch her, know she still lived.

Each day he checked the door, and each day it stayed maddeningly closed.

The more days past, the more his anxiety mounted. He took it with him to bed and in the morning it was breathing down his neck before he opened his eyes.

Focusing on his job was insanely difficult. He preferred to be a stalker at the bridge. Then he felt he was doing *something.*

Over a figment of your imagination! Ram's voice, a-*gain.*

His eyes flicked to the corn maze, finally finished yesterday, amidst fifty-million other duties leading up to the Fall Festival.

It was the orphanage's most important fundraiser of the year. And here he was, hiding in his room, neglecting his chores. *Like one of the bloody adolescents.*

Dr. Linkler wouldn't attend this year—the old man was having trouble walking…so they'd conference call him after it was done to discuss the proceeds.

A book slipped off his bed, hitting the ground with a loud thud.

He froze, expecting a childish call to crack the

silence.

Ram knocked and poked his head in; his eyes widened at the piles of books. Truman knew he was counting them.

"True, this is beyond obsession. Over what? Some personification of a woman you've invented?"

Truman ground his teeth together. "I *did not* invent her. I shouldn't have told you. I don't give a crap if you don't believe me; I have more important things to worry about."

Ram's dark eyebrows knitted. "Yes, you do. Like the Fall Harvest Festival today. Like all the money it raises for the orphanage. *Like our paychecks.* Like that new little boy upstairs, who seems to only respond *to you*, not me? Like all the other children we have here. Like the date you have with Antonia tonight."

"Bullocks. I completely forgot about her. I made that months ago. I'm canceling."

"No, you-are-not canceling. It's been eons since you were on a date. You're going. Close that computer and help me with the insanity downstairs. We vowed to do this together, did we not?"

Ram's voice was tired and his eyes were bleary. He looked a decade older today.

He'd been selfish, leaving Ram with the brunt of the work.

They'd promised to do it together—to give a few children a shot at a happy childhood. Unlike their own.

"I'm sorry. I've been selfish," he said, snapping the laptop closed. "I've just… never felt this way. Ever."

Ram rolled his eyes, but they softened a fraction. "Typical you. Could never fall in love in a normal way, with a normal person."

"No, that would definitely be boring."

* * *

10:00 a.m.

Truman slid into the pantry, hiding. He pressed his forehead against the cool wall, escaping the chaos, searching his head for any remaining-shreds of patience. He wiped his forehead with his sleeve. The calliope music from the carnival filtered under the door—reminding him his respite was limited.

I'm bloody losing it.

He flipped open his phone and texted Antonia. A total cop-out.

Have to cancel. Sorry. Something came up. True.

He hoped it would be enough and she didn't just show on his porch—that woman did not take no for an answer.

He hit the 'send' button and startled as the pantry door slid open.

Tiny Andrew stared up at him; his huge, black eyes questioning. "Truman, are you coming? We don't have much time."

"Yes, so right you are, lad."

Outside, the barnyard was a flurry of activity. Children and volunteers streaked back and forth on fast forward.

It would be comical if he weren't so utterly stressed.

Ram strode toward him, his face grim. "Are you ready? Cruella De Ville cometh."

He turned, indicating a tall, grey haired woman, distinctly out of place in the barnyard.

Her long, shapely legs teetered on high heels, her designer bag dangling from red-hot nails. Her new tightened skin belied her current face-lift.

Ram chortled. "The devil *does* wear Prada."

Truman dropped his voice. "And Gucci. That bag she's clutching costs as much as our mortgage."

"What's that expression about biting the hand that…."

Truman cleared his throat as the woman arrived.

She studiously ignored Ram.

"Truman! So wonderful to see you again. Are you ready to give me the tour?" She extended a hand to him.

Truman cringed. Ram intentionally sicked the older woman on him. She fancied him—was in love with his accent.

"Yes, mum."

Ram winked behind her back. Truman returned with an I'll-deal-with-you-later look.

"Ram, I will speak with you when we are finished," she added with a flippant wave.

Truman led her into the orphanage, beginning with the ground floor and the O.T. clinic, explaining the different types of patients seen there. He opened the sliding doors for her to peek inside.

"We have loads of kids with sensory integration problems, autism spectrum disorders, Down's Syndrome, and many feeding kids."

"What do you mean by *feeding kids*?"

"Children who are on tubes to eat for a variety of different reasons. It is our job to figure out why, and to try and help them regain that ability—if they're able."

"I see. Sounds challenging."

Truman laughed; it had a very rough edge.

"Yes, you have no idea. Many of the kids we get here are from terrible homes. Were never cared for, have attachment disorders. They come in unbathed. Many end up in foster care."

Like me.

"Like your facility?"

"Yes."

He led her out into the sun, thankful to leave the clinic.

The sun warmed his face, and the sounds of children's laughter split his lips into a reluctant smile. His shoulders relaxed as he stared at the carnival.

The neighboring children's home, one for girls, had brought a busload. Truman stared at the bright colors and ponytails trickling off the bus. It felt so foreign amidst his daily deluge of baseball bats, action figures and ultimate fighter re-enactments. Their house mother, Jo, led the way, as the girl's followed in a queue, reminding him of ducklings.

Sophie, his favorite, waved vigorously from the back of the line. She charged over, breaking ranks. Jo rolled her eyes, but halted the procession.

"Where's my booth?" she said excitedly.

"Go find Ram. It's all set up."

She turned to bolt, but he caught her shoulder. "Manners, Sophie."

She gave Mrs. Simon a cursory glance. "Hello!" and took off.

Truman chuckled. "Sorry, she's a little excitable."

He watched Ram position her behind her booth.

A few of his little ones played tag in the mini-hay bale maze. Ram had gone all out this year, renting a proper carousel. The calliope music tinkled throughout the thoroughfare.

He led the way, walking Cruella past a massive pumpkin patch, where orange orbs of every shape and breadth littered the ground as numerous as the fall leaves.

Patrons arrived in droves now, and a man hoisted his wee girl onto a giant pumpkin, where her legs dangled in the air. Her mother snapped a perfectly-posed shot.

His gut pinched in a familiar emotion. *Jealousy.* Although he took joy in matching happy families, deep down, he envied them. *All he'd ever wanted was normal.* It was his way of coping; to heal these children by giving them what he'd never had.

"What is that contraption?" Mrs. Simon asked, pointing at a tall, wooden tower.

"That is in case of emergency, for the corn maze."

He spoke quickly in response to her concerned look. "In three years, we haven't had a problem yet."

Fall chrysanthemums in shades of orange, yellow and deepest maroon sat upon hay bales throughout the yard.

They arrived at the hot and cold cider shanty. "This is David and Ethan, our high-schoolers. They only have one more year with us."

"Good day, boys."

"David is going on to trade school, and Ethan…isn't sure yet. He's considering staying on with us as a hand."

Truman shuffled her past the row of kiosks, often

reaching over to steady her as her stilettos rolled over a rock.

The next shanty had glow-sticks for sale, manned by waifish Sophie. She gave Mrs. Simon what Truman recognized as her most-winning smile. Sophie was determined to be an actress. "Good day, Mum," she said, in a spot-on imitation of Truman's Scottish accent.

Ms. Simon laughed delightedly, her eyes flicking to Truman's. "Why child, that is excellent."

"Sophie will be doing the costumed story-telling tonight in the barn, by candlelight. It's one of our biggest sellers for the festival."

As they turned to go, he shot her a wink. She really was his favorite. Such a corker.

Passing the pumpkin pie booth, they reached the barn which bordered the cornfield.

"Inside, we have the horses, and I'll be doing a hay-ride later, and of course the maze-which is a huge undertaking for two of us. In the winter, we also do sleigh rides. I bought a buggy from the local Amish. So, you see, we are doing our best to fund the orphanage on our own. Of course, your donations are tremendously helpful to offset the costs for the children."

Ms. Simon shoo'ed a fly buzzing near her ear. "Do you ride, Truman?"

"Yes, mum. I teach the children to ride, and they also are involved in many chores around the place to teach them responsibility."

"Tell me about the maze."

His eyes drifted across the stocks. "The maze is five acres across. We have bridges placed in the four corners—north, south, east, west. It has two emergency exits for children who get frustrated."

A shrill, feminine scream rent the air.

They both froze, mid-stride.

His heart leapt on a wave of adrenaline. His legs tensed, ready to run.

"Help! Help me!"

"Bollocks." He whispered the word on an exhale.

A teen-aged girl busted out the maze's mouth and charged them. Her hair swirled in the wind and her face constricted, contorting; her eyes wild with fear.

"My little brother, I've lost him in the corn. I can hear him screaming, but I can't find him anywhere! He says there's something in there!"

Truman's eyes met Ram's, mirroring his panic. "Ram, get up in the tower with a walkie-talkie. I'm going in."

Truman bolted after the teen and followed her down the green paths, and was quickly swallowed by the corn.

* * *

The wind whips up and I shiver, staring at the Putnam house, which looks as bleak and weather-worn as I feel.

My legs feel leaden, as if the cold has seeped in and frozen them to the marrow.

My cracked hands itch and sting; when I curl my fingers toward my palm, it feels like ice cracking.

Truman. My chores are woefully behind. I find myself staring stupidly, thinking of him. The door will not permit me entry. My mind whispers he is a manifestation of the Man in Black. Our Bible sermon spoke of the devil appearing as an angel of light.

His name summons a cornflower-blue word in my mind, similar to the color of his eyes. Fear fills my chest, but a new, selfish *need* rages, and my hands shake, a forest-fire burning up my chest, threatening to consume me. To stay with him, be by his side.

Living is harder now. Now that I've felt something other than fear.

I ache with loneliness; as if my self, once content with scraps of joy, had now seen and felt a bounty, and would not accept less.

It vacated my heart; I can almost hear its echoes, rattling around inside my hollow chest.

My fingers twitch in recollection; to run them through his thick, dark hair, smooth away those worried lines on his forehead. He is too young for such lines.

When he looks at me-he sees past my brave façade.

He understands me—cares not if I am orphaned, poor and *different*. And come with the load of rearing my brother.

Decision slams a door in my heart.

I shall run. Any place be better than Salem.

The crushing weight on my heart lifts. I've made up my mind. How to convince John?

Screams and shouts bring me back. I turn and run, crunching through the knee-deep snow back toward the Putnam house.

Anne's screeching voice echoes into the night, and gooseflesh sprouts from scalp to toe.

"Mother! Call Constable Corwin! He be afflicting

me!"

I step inside as Anne Jr. slumps to the floor, muscles twitching as if an invisible seamstress jabs and pulls at a million different points on her pale skin.

John stands aghast in the middle of the room, hands protecting his ears.

Anne's head whips up to stare at Mercy, who looks as mortified as John.

"Mercy Lewis, confess. You told me, John confided in you that he sees shapes and pictures when music plays. If *that* is not the work of the Man in Black, I do not know what is! He speaks to him through the music! That be why he can draw so well."

Mercy's eyes brim and she turns to John, shaking her head. "Oh, John. I am so sorry! I should not have told her!"

Dread and bile fill my mouth, and my limbs shake with a violence to rival Anne's.

Anne Sr. stares at John, her gaze lighting like a match-struck.

"John Montague, be you in league with the dark one? Have you signed his book?"

The hornets whir to life, and I see the word, death, flash, blinking red in my head.

"No!" I scream, launching myself at Ms. Putnam's feet with outstretched arms. Blocking John.

"Please, Mum, John is an innocent—*incapable* of deceit. Of lying, even!"

John opens his mouth, and stutters. My heart bleeds in my chest at the thought of him gone from me. Back to the dirt, with the rest of my family.

"I l-l-love God, Mum. I would *never* do wrong."

Anne Sr.'s eyes are hard as flint. She juts a finger

toward the door. "Mercy. Go and fetch Constable Corwin."

"No! No! No!"

I fly in front of John, spreading my arms wide. "You shall *never* take him! Or hang him! You shall have to kill me first!"

A blinding red rage grips me. I will hurt her now, if she's so daft to try and touch him.

Mercy stands frozen, hands covering her face, appalled at the circumstance she's created.

Mrs. Putnam shrieks, stamping her foot on the floor at my insubordination. "*Now,* Mercy!"

Mercy bolts, eyes cast down, out the door.

Anne Jr. continues her theatrics, writhing and making strangled sounds from the floor. I've learned, when Anne's eyes roll and jiggle the fit be real, but now, every once and again she steals a glance at me. She's pretending.

I grasp John's hand, hurtling toward the front door.

"Where do you think you are going?" Anne Sr. screams, a bit of spittle flying. Her eyes are mad. A rabid animal.

I yell over my shoulder, "My brother is innocent, same as most of the accused in Salem."

Years of hatred, encased in years of silent servitude, crack open and overflow from my mouth.

I stop, scowling back at the writhing girl. "Sarah Good, a poor beggar-woman. Tiny Dorcas Good, Anne? Bewitching you? *Dorcas is but four years old.* What could that child do to you? You're right the devil is in Salem, but it's in his works, not the Man in Black. Selfishness, greed, *and lies.*"

"You will both hang!" Anne Sr. shrieks.

She lunges, grasping for my frock. I twirl out of her reach. Her desperate fingers clutch to find purchase on the fabric.

I wrangle out of her grasp and haul John toward freedom.

I kick open the door with my boot-heel and plunge him out through the thigh-high snow, slogging headlong across the yard for the cornfield.

"Please, open. Oh, dear merciful heavens let it open," I whisper over and over as we charge into the withering, yellowed rows.

Chapter 12

Truman bolted through the corn, half-screaming into the walkie-talkie. “Ram, can you see him ennawhere?”

His reply crackled with static. “No, not yet.”

Turning, he searched above the corn tops for the observation tower. It was built precisely for such occasions, but never used in the past three years of the maze.

“Try to send out a call to the other talkies.”

He skidded to a stop in front of the first one, mounted on a stalk. It was Ethan’s job to go through the maze once a week and to check the batteries. With the sheer size of it, they’d devised this back-up plan. Eight different talkies were planted throughout the leafy puzzle to lead children to the exits. Like an auditory trail of breadcrumbs.

A few rows over, the crackle of the Victrola started.

“Oh, please, not now.”

Ram’s voice sounded from the stalk. “Can you hear me? Tommy?”

Truman depressed the button on the mounted talkie. “I’m at number one, it works. Keep calling him and keep trying. I so do not want to call in a ‘copter; it will be terrible press."

"I've got the older kids going out in pairs, starting at the four corner entrances, closing in toward the center."

A rustling to the north caught his ear. He bolted, changing directions.

A beat up trainer disappeared into a neighboring row ahead. Disembodied crying erupted directly beside his ear. He whirled, tripping. It faded in and out, like a stereo turned up then down. His head swiveled, trying to keep up with the circling sound.

The snuffling rose to howling. Howling like an animal in pain.

The raspy voice surrounded him, a puff of breath into his ear.

He whirled. His heart throbbed, skipping a beat.

Nothing, no one anywhere.

"Wot is going on now? I dunna have time for this!"

Truman flew to the spot where the shoe had evaporated, following the pinnacle of the wailing.

He halted, dumbstruck.

A section of corn shook to life; the stalks collapsed, falling one over the other like rows of dominos, resulting in a tiny crop circle.

The circle darkened as the bright blue sky above it faded to black. A circular room materialized, dusty and lined with books from floor to ceiling. A rocking chair creaked before a blazing fire, which blasted his face with heat.

His heart went apoplectic, then gunned into overdrive, as if someone'd injected it with pure adrenaline.

His legs quivered, preparing to bolt.

"I-I…." No words would come. Would fit.

A small boy crouched in the center, his arms wrapped about his knees in a tight ball. A book lay at his side, *Oliver Twist*. His body gently rocked, as he tried to console himself. Tears cut dirty tracks down his cheeks.

Odd, he doesn't show a color.

Fear and empathy warred in his chest. He hesitated, foot poised to step inside the circle.

Empathy won. He stepped into the darkened library. The door slammed shut, and the cornfield evaporated. His dry throat clicked as he opened his mouth.

The Victrola crackled to life. Judy's voice again. This time skipping "…that's where, that's where, that's where…."

"You'll find me," he whispered, completing the sentence.

A burning, paternal protection swelled his heart.

"Are you all right? I'm 'ere, now. I'll take you home, boy." He was but five feet away from the cowering child when a chill scurried up his back like a smattering of spiders.

His heart leapt, plummeted, and lodged somewhere near his stomach.

The boy's hair, dirty and unkempt, had a familiar cowlick. His tiny hands kneaded a filthy stuffed dog; its once brown-coat was now black with use.

Pain shot through his nose and a bitter taste filled his mouth. Signs that tears were brewing.

The pain-fear sensation shot through his groin. *He knew those trainers.* He'd worn them till they rubbed raw blisters on the tips of his toes, till social services finally got him a new pair.

And Oliver Twist. Reading kept me sane. Becoming part of the story was my only escape.

It was *him*. A younger him.

Bottled pain—kept at bay by years of practice—popped open, bubbling back into his consciousness.

He dropped to his knees beside the boy, sobbing. Reaching out, he tried to gather him into his arms. To give his younger self the comfort he so desperately desired. To tell him one day, it would be all right. He wouldn't be lonely.

A shrill blast, like a freight train, swept up about his head. The entire circle rotated, like a dizzying merry-go-round. Its revolutions spiraled faster and faster till with a pop, the boy and the library disappeared.

Cramming his eyes closed, he waited for the spinning in his head to quiet.

Ram's voice came through the talkie, uttering a string of curses. "Truman! Where are you? I can't see you in there! Answer me *right now* or I'm coming in."

True stumbled, one foot collapsing as his ankle twisted from the trembling. "I'm here. I thought I found him…but I didn't."

"What are you babbling about?" Ram's voice was quavering. No doubt, vivid images of their dream being shut down were playing in his mind, as the identical scenes flashed behind Truman's eyes.

A great, grumbling hiss erupted, filling the air. He wheeled toward the sound. A myriad of bodiless voices erupted in a strange sing-song harmony.

They surrounded him, like a circle. He twirled on

the spot, head revolving. Nothing. Just the stalks swaying in the summer breeze.

The a capella harmony rose, getting closer and fading, getting closer and fading; as if the voices whispered in his ear, then darted away. His head rocked with vertigo.

"*Truu*-man," a sad voice crooned, rising above the humming.

His gut contracted as if sucker-punched.

The talkie bounced off the ground as his hands flew to the sides of his head. To protect his mind.

I am having a psychotic episode. I've finally snapped.

"The silly boy is to the South," the whisper said. Its voice was a growl and a rasp; a horrid union of splintering tree branches and the hissing of wasps. "Mind the girl, she needs you. Her hourglass is almost empty."

The chorus of voices held one long, droning note, and cut off like the closing of a maestro's fist. The whispering grew fainter, moving away, and disappeared with another sucking pop.

"Truman! Truman! I can see you now, what was that I heard?"

He bent, retrieving the talkie. His shaking hand bashed it against his jaw. He depressed the button. Every movement was labored, to keep plugged into reality.

"I dunno. I'm so glad you bloody heard it. I thought I was losing me mind. Use the binoculars; they said he's to the South."

"They…spoke to you? I just heard some freaky-weird sounds."

"Yeah. I'm a freak-magnet." His chest convulsed with laughter. It felt wrong, hysterical.

"I see him! Head down there, I'll transmit to the talkie down there and try to keep him still."

Within ten minutes Truman was carrying the shaking boy out of the exit of the maze to a waiting camera crew, courtesy of the local news station. Flashbulbs exploded, making instant spots dance before his eyes.

Ram waited behind the mob of reporters, looking irritated. He shrugged his shoulders helplessly.

A microphone was thrust two inches from Truman's lips. He considered biting it.

"How is the boy doing?"

"He will be fine, just a little scared is all." He handed the boy off to the waiting arms of his teenage sister.

A car screeched to a halt in the barnyard, sending gravel flying. A woman busted out of the passenger side door and bolted toward them. "Billy! On my heavens, Billy!"

"There are voices in the corn," the boy whispered, so low only Truman and his sister heard him. The girl eyed him warily.

Truman held up his hands. "That's it folks, show's over!" He and Ram motioned to the older boys to assist in escorting the media off the premises.

Truman searched for Cruella in the crowd, but she was nowhere. His gut thumped with another pulse of worry.

"I think it's fine. I think she'll still donate." Ram had reassured him later. But his stomach was not a believer.

Twilight fell, and with it, the milling festival guests finally departed. He'd thought it wise to cancel the story readings in the barn, much to Sophie's outrage. She never missed a chance to perform.

"Truman," she whined, "It's ridiculous! You know how good my readings are!"

"Tomorrow night, I promise, love. Ram and I are spent, even if the rest of you aren't. My nerves are frayed like I've just had a lobotomy."

When the girl reluctantly let Jo shuffle her onto the bus, he stood and paced in front of the porch till it was out of sight.

"Settle down, Scotty. It's over now, and Cruella was easily placated."

"That's not the point!" he screamed. His carefully jailed emotions busted free of their incarceration. "Our whole dream could have been destroyed today! There is *something* in the corn! Don't reason it away, Dr. Strangelove—you bloody well heard them too!"

He bit his lip and squinted toward the corn maze.

He strode over to the barn, plucking a flashlight off the shelf. Its strong beam cut a line of light through the thick blackness of the barnyard.

"What are you doing? We have at least three kids to ready for bed."

"Get Sunny to stay. Tell her its overtime."

He heard Ram's exasperated cursing as he jogged into the corn.

* * *

My knees go weak at the sound. *Dogs.* Not far behind. I clap my hands over my mouth to stifle the scream clawing up my throat.

I whisper, "Run John!"

I grab his hand, and pull him, weaving through the stalks. Words shoot through my head like musket fire of emotions and color.

Doomed, fight, save him.

"Verity, I'm frightened. They will hang me!"

"Oh John, oh my love! Keep running! Do not look back!"

A loud, booming voice rises over the barks. "Verity and John Montague, you are commanded to surrender on suspicion of witchcraft! If you cease to flee, the court will take this into consideration!"

John halts; his eyes trusting and clear.

"*No,* John." I shake his shoulders. "Think of poor old Rebecca Nurse. She did nothing wrong. They lie to catch us."

If I die, even if I don't hang, he is lost. He will always see the best in people, even at their worst. I yank harder on his elbow.

Gratefulness opens a yawning hole in my chest. The bridge appears in the swirling snow ahead.

"Oh, thank Providence!"

Clomping up to the apex, I push him across it—*and run down the other side.*

The door does not open. Same moon. Same cold night.

"Oh, no! Oh, no!"

My mind is shutting down. Giving up. I see little bits of my sanity flying off in all directions like a spinning wheel. With each revolution, I am going. Madness is very close.

The hornets. The hornets. They fill my head. I

stick a finger in my ear and shriek, swearing I feel its crunchy insect body escaping.

I pull John back up to the center of the bridge and wail, "Please, please help us! Do not let us die!"

The dogs' yelp so close the hair on my arms stands.

"Verity…" John's lips move, but no sounds come out. For once, we don't need words as our eyes lock. Our fear is a synchronous, heaving being we both feel.

We are about to die.

For being different.

My legs collapse and I hit the hard wood of the bridge. My courage dries up and I sob, grasping at John's pant leg. I feel his fingers touch the top of my head.

Then, a disembodied hand appears, its fingers fervently searching.

* * *

The night is beyond black. Every light in the orphanage is finally out. The lighted windows extinguished one at a time over the past hour. The house reminds him of an old man, who's reluctant, fluttering eyes finally relented to sleep.

The flashlight's beam cut through the rows, bouncing in time with his jogging.

Tonight feels…wrong. Something is up.

It's as if the night is holding its breath, waiting, watching.

Something's wrong, all right; aside from my mentally abusive job, that I'm emotionally retarded and almost lost all the funding for the house.

Waves of luminescent color, red and green, seep from the corn's rows, like the whole field is under some blinding, celestial black-light.

He hears them. Those bloody bluebirds. Why are they out at night? *Abnormal.*

His heart rockets and he walks toward the sound. His mouth waters with anxiety.

His mind nags this is one of those awful, *defining moments.*

An *explosion* of blue erupts around him. Streaks made of bluebirds whiz past his eyes.

He stumbles, their unexpected attack causing vertigo. They're so thick, he's blinded.

A tornado of revolving feathers starts at his feet and rises to encircle his head.

Their trilling songs are too high. He winces and covers his ears.

And he's alone again.

They take flight, like one collective mind, into the cornrows.

He feels the compulsion. To follow. He obeys, his feet digging in without his mind's permission.

Weaving through the rows, they're leading to the north bridge.

Longing and apprehension and agitation congeal in his stomach.

Bits of music waft through the corn and with each a new wave of emotion, and colors.

A cello calls from far away and is answered by a violin, like two loons exchanging vows.

Pain is everywhere. It's palpable, like a breeze—it fills the air like a heady mist.

"What is *this place?"*

The voice of the corn, which is young and old, male and female, multi-layered and clotted—erupts beside his ear. "A place to right the wrongs."

His breath puffs out in mini-gasps and his legs automatically bolt further inside.

Another round of music, from the south. A drum and fife core. The snare drum and piccolo call out a staccato military march.

Then, what undoubtedly must be *his* song begins again. Judy Garland's voice trickles through his blood, chilling it.

Verity is in trouble.

He knows it, can feel it to his marrow.

He launches to a run, winding in and out of the paths, hurtling downed stalks—his only thought, *the bridge. The bridge.*

On the apex, Verity crouches, partially visible through the translucent, flexuous door.

Her mismatched eyes are wild, and her hands pat the entrance, as if searching for an opening. A young, gangly boy stands alongside her, crying. *Shaking.* With the most pathetic shade of despondent orange. As he moves, his color lingers, sticking to the air, like a comet's tail.

Truman drops to his knees, feeling along the cold, hard surface of the door. It's surface stings, like freezing snow, but he presses his fingertips harder, searching.

Verity's sobbing and his heart is fracturing in his chest. Her face appears an inch away—but the door…hundreds of years compressed into the small space between them.

Glistening, fat teardrop's bead on her red lashes.

They dangle then fall, in a strange slow-motion descent before disappearing into the snow.

Her mouth pulls a cruel grimace; her lips a frantic trembling mess.

"Oh, Verity."

And he hears them. Dogs. They are after them.

Hatred sparks, flaring in his chest at the gross injustice; it spirals round in his head, gaining momentum, till all rational thought is incinerated.

He cocks his fist, slamming into the door, *over and over*. Blood trickles between his knuckles; he grunts at the snap as one breaks.

Through the door, the heightened sound of barking dogs. Tracking dogs.

The realization strikes like a bolt of fire.

"No. You *will* live."

He rams his shoulder into the ice-door, grimacing at the pain in his broken fingers. He slams it, again and again, feeling the hot-cold pain sear his shoulder as the ice rips it open.

Finally, the door budges, fracturing down the middle; his fingers part the cold, cracking it wide-open.

It shudders as it slides; like a displaced, animated glacier.

His hand thrusts through the crack, his fingers frantically searching for her.

Truman's fingertips brush a coarse texture; like a burlap feed-sack.

The air-door turns flexuous-a rectangular outline, shimmering in the night sky. It ripples as it melts, like the surface of a pool of water.

Through it, Verity's moon appears, bright and full

in the night sky.

The door phases again, changing to mist. It revolves and the sound of her sobs and the barks intensify.

"Verity! Where are you?" Her figure was dimming and brightening in time with the door's clarity.

Truman grimaces and plunges both hands into the liquefied air, groping. His fingers find her coarse, long hair.

Her face turns away. She's giving up. She turns, ready to bolt off the bridge, away from the dogs. *Away from him.*

Gritting his teeth, his fingers reach for her and slip. He lurches forward in panic, grasping her dress with both hands, he heaves.

Her tiny body flies through the door, landing in a heap on his chest, flattening them both against the bridge.

The color surrounding her is horror-personified; black, spiraling clouds of flashing darkness.

"Truman! Truman!" her hands convulse with pain. "My brother, get my brother!"

"What?"

He turns as the door phases from translucent to transparent. The young man crouches on the other side of the bridge.

Truman swallows, vaulting forward. *Oh, his color…*

The boy's fear was a pulsing, shuddering, multi-hued monster.

A crowd of men and snarling dogs arrive simultaneously, hesitating at the bridge's bottom.

One man in the crowd locks eyes with Truman—their gaze holds for a brief second, but he looks away, terrified.

"What devilry be this?" Corwin screams. Veins pop in his neck. "Where has your sister gone? Left you to hang for her deeds?"

"No! No! She is not a witch!" the boy says. He throws back his trembling shoulders.

His eyes flick to the revolving door. He gives no other indication that he's seen it. Protecting her.

Truman rams the door harder, summoning all his strength. Another finger-bone snaps. The door's surface glows and glitters; hard as diamonds once again.

Verity's ragged breathing catches behind him.

"John Montague. You are hereby charged with witchcraft, and will be tried before your peers."

"No! No!" Verity stumbles in sightless circles.

Her wail freezes his blood. It is primal and maternal, as if by taking John, they have excised her beating heart from her chest.

She bends in half, crumpling into a fetal position.

In desperation, he slams the door again, knowing it's useless.

It was a solid, transparent door to nowhere. His shoulder screams in pain.

She lifts her red eyes, and begins crawling toward the door, pleading, "Please, take me. Not him. Please, merciful Father."

It's a window, now, not a door.

"John, no, not my John," Verity sobs.

He lowers his head, and rams it again; the sound of tinkling glass echoes through the corn.

Shimmering slivers of light shower down on them, disappearing before they strike the ground.

Truman tumbles as the door shatters, vaulting forward, sliding down the other side of the bridge as the connection broke; the door disappearing with a clap of thunder.

He turns to see Verity weeping into her hands. Her eyes roll back in her head and she collapses onto the wood.

In the sky, *one moon* shines clear and bright.

Chapter 13

Verity's unconscious form felt warm against his chest. He weaved through the stalks, his only thought—to get her inside. His legs pumped hard and fast, burning with the pace.

The realization hit when he spied the orphanage's roof.

How will I explain this? His eyes dropped to her face. *Explain her?*

He mentally rifled through a million explanations and lies. Panic expanded, filling his chest like a helium balloon.

Her color, which outlined her like a separate living, breathing being, pulsed a weak purple. Beneath, a red-hot core revealed her terror.

Verity's chest heaved; even unconscious, her terror remained.

He reached the corn's mouth, and cut across the barnyard.

Ram was waiting on the porch.

He shot out of his chair, a look of complete incomprehension on his face.

His dark eyes widened, taking in Verity's provincial clothing. "How? No. It's impossible."

Truman gave him a terse nod. "I told you she was

real."

Emotions flickered through his eyes. "I'm going to tell Sunny to keep the kids out of the way…till…we figure out a story. The converted guest loft in the barn—True, take her there."

"Brilliant. That's why you're the doc."

Instead of smiling, Ram looked as if he might vomit. He rushed inside the orphanage without another word.

Truman sped toward the barn, barely breaking stride as he kicked the door open. He clambered up the stairs to the apartment, his nose wrinkling at the musty smell.

He eased her onto the bed.

Verity's skin was milk-white, and her lips parted as if in a dreamlike kiss. Desire spread through his mind and body as he stared at her.

He bit his lip.

He turned away, murmuring, "Focus, you're pathetic. She's bloody unconscious."

Her dress was polka-dotted with mud. He stared at her dirt-caked boots and set to unlacing them.

Glimpses of her brother popped into his head as guilt ripped his conscience to shreds.

He swallowed, remembering his bravery. And selflessness.

His lanky body shook all over—but he stood firm, against a mob of witch-crazed zealots.

Proclaiming his and Verity's innocence. Truman swallowed the lump in his throat.

The lad couldn't be more than fifteen.

How long would he have? How long did a trial take in those days?

The steps creaked. Someone was coming.

Sunny appeared at the door, her dark eyes taut with worry.

"Oh, Sun. I need your help. She's filthy. If I get her into the tub, could you…?"

Sunny's eyes flicked from Verity to his face, back and forth like a cornered animal. "Is she Amish?"

"No…."

Her expression darkened.

"Sure, True. Anything for you. But you have some serious explaining to do. I'm not going to be charged with some sort of felony or anything, right? Please, tell me she's eighteen."

"I didn't kidnap her." He busted out laughing, but stopped abruptly when she continued to stare.

"It is a long, difficult-to-believe story, but I'll tell you everything. If you're sure you want me to. Sometimes ignorance is bliss."

Sunny's eyebrow rose. "Lose my right to plead the fifth, huh? I dunno. I'll tell you after I hear it." She eased Verity into her arms and walked toward the bathroom without another word.

Strange, new feelings bombarded him. Fear, married to a protective surge so strong, he pressed his fists against his forehead.

A fierce love—raw and savage—gutted his heart.

Verity was so innocent and so uniquely beautiful, inside and out, like no other woman he'd ever met.

"I'll protect you, Verity," he murmured.

Sunny poked her head out the bathroom door. "What did you say?"

"Nothing."

* * *

John held his breath as Constable Corwin led him into the dank room. His boots clomped, echoing off the walls as they entered the witch dungeon. Flickering candlelight danced across the pools of water on the dark stones, shifting like a million blinking eyes. A shrill sound jabbed into his eardrum like a knife. He covered his ears. That pitch could only be one creature.

Rats. Loads of them.

His exceptionally acute hearing registered the clicks of thousands of tiny nails scraping across the stone floor.

“Here is where ye shall await trial, John.”

John swallowed and tried not to weep but felt the familiar burn in his nose and the resulting water fill his eyes. Tears of fear leaked out. Panic bloated his mind, screaming at him to strike the man—*to flee*.

He began to rock.

The cell before him was impossibly small; there was no chance of lying down. It was the exact size of an upright coffin. If he attempted to sit, his long legs would jut out the bars.

Corwin touched his back, sliding him in. The jail door clanged and closed with a loud, final click.

A *glut* of emotion squeezed his chest. A numbing fear rose, making his limbs feel disconnected, uncontrollable. They flailed uselessly.

He whimpered. Sliding down the wall, he wrapped himself into a protective ball and permitted the tears to come.

A younger boy stood beside Corwin. He did not

know his name.

"Excuse my frankness, sir. But, John has always been different." The boy's eyes flicked to John on the floor of the coffin-cell. "I don't think he is capable of malice, let alone maleficia."

"That will be for the court to decide, son. Sometimes, the company we keep condemns us. His sister is surely a witch."

The boy's face was skeptical.

"Examine the evidence—those mismatched eyes, her flaming hair. Now this news *he* somehow sees shapes within music—undeniably this be the devil's handiwork—"

The constable's words cut through John's protective bubble, reviving his immobile limbs.

His stomach clenched, his ears rang with his hatred.

Rage, *which he so carefully controlled*, always avoiding it like a leper, *took control of him*. He leapt to stand, shoving his face against the bars, snarling through them like a wild dog.

"Verity-be-not-a-witch! She's the most loving, caring young woman in the world. All of *you* shall be guilty before God for hanging innocents! Look around you! These be people you've known for years!" Spittle flew from his mouth, splattering Corwin's chin.

A renewed chorus of weeping filled the witch dungeon.

Tituba's dark eyes bore into him from across the room; her small body in an identical tiny coffin cell.

The poor got the smallest cells. And while the rich were afforded larger accommodations—but *all* were made to *pay* for the food and lodging time in jail.

Leaving servants and orphans as permanent inmates—without the assistance of fortune on the outside.*

Money, the root of all things injurious.

Many were dying, rotting on the cell floors.

Constable Corwin held up a hand as if to ward off his thoughts. "Let's go, Tom, and leave the ravings of this lunatic for his fellow witches."

Tom grimaced but followed.

John felt his rage reorganize and twist into something desperate. *"Look at the faces of these people!"*

All were staring. It was, no doubt, the most words they'd ever heard him put together. He guessed many thought him mute.

"Martha Corey? She has been in this cursed place five months! Accused because that malicious pack of girls say a yellow bird suckled betwixt her fingers? Because they *claim*, her specter haunted them, asking them to sign the devil's book? I could create such fiction right now—against you!"

His chest felt heavy with the unfamiliar emotion.

"Elizabeth Proctor!" His finger jutted out between the bars, pointing across the dungeon. "She is pregnant. Have you no mercy? You incarcerate in the name of God. *God* would show mercy!"

Tom's face was fearful. "John, calm thyself." His eyes glanced warily at Constable Corwin's face, which flushed a deeper red with each of John's accusations.

"Dorcas Good—she's been here seven months. *She-is-a-child!*"

The tiny girl, chained to the wall, began to cry and fretfully look about at the sound of her name.

She was clearly mad now.

"These should have considered the consequences, before signing away their lives to the dark one!" Corwin said, with a sweeping gesture of his hand. "Pray, answer me this, John. How does thou explain the palsies, and the dropping fits? The vomiting and odd contortions of so many afflicted in this village, if not for the devil's design."

"I saw one of the dogs that was hanged. *It took ill*, sir. It's afflictions reminded of d-distemper." His voice broke on the last word, and with it, his will.

Corwin looked thoughtful for a moment, then harrumphed, stomping toward the exit. Tom followed in his wake, eyes downcast. He murmured, "Only God and time will tell."

The dungeon door clanged shut, and a fresh chorus of wails sang through the fetid air. John slumped back into a ball, rocking, closing his eyes, covering his ears to the pain.

Chapter 14

My eyes refuse to open. My fingertips find the pulsing spot they used to inhabit, and rub furiously. I open the lids a slit, and immediately wish I hadn't. The light is pure pain—a needle spearing my eyeball, trying to pop it from its socket. This pain is familiar.

I don't welcome it like an old friend; I wrinkle my nose and know I must ride out this unwanted visitor inside my skull. The pain has one good trait. It vanquishes the hornets. The cowards vacate at the first sign of it.

I hear the bed creak, and it depresses beside me as someone sits down. The throb in my head is muted because of this bed. I've never felt a place so comforting. I picture myself lying amid wispy clouds as I roll toward the unseen form.

They must be very wealthy. Perhaps I could be their servant.

My mind searches. My thoughts befuddled—trying to recall my most recent memory. Then it rushes back, vomiting up images.

The men. John. The bridge. I whimper.

"Are you all right?" a low voice whispers. I'd recognize it anywhere now. My heart immediately hammers in my chest.

Pain like a hatchet if I open my eyes…

I decide a glimpse be worth it. Familiar, almond-shaped, bright-blue eyes consider me. *Kind eyes*. He has a calming presence, as I haven't felt in many years. His hands are anxious, folded in front of his face as he stares overtop them.

No man has ever regarded me such. It seems *he cannot look away*. His expression reminds me of men gazing at a master's paintings; awe and desire and longing. *For me?*

"My head—it pains me beyond speech."

"What does it feel like? Can you describe it?"

"A pain behind my eye and the light-how is there so much light?" I sit up quickly, glancing outside at the black night. I am surrounded by strange machines which drive back the darkness. "Where be the candles? What devilry be this?"

My head screams in protest from the quick move to sitting. I cry out, and silence it by sinking my teeth into my bottom lip.

"It sounds like a migraine. Please, Verity, lay down."

My mind flashes a picture of my brother. The panic resumes as the familiar tingling fingers of fear desert my face and wrap around my neck. I gasp with the feeling.

"John, oh my John. I must return to him."

I slide my feet off the bed, trying to stand. I feel my knee hit the floor before I realize I am falling. My hands slap against the floor, narrowly rescuing my head. The pain behind my eyes behind my eyes roars to an exquisite, pulsing intensity.

It culminates behind my eye. My stomach seizes,

my head imploding. "Oh, no." Vomit erupts from my mouth, surrounding me.

"Oh, Truman, I am so terribly sorry." I freeze, irrationally awaiting the whip's sting across my back. My mind spews out memories of public floggings.

I keep my eyes shut, coward that I am—but the silence is so loud…I open them.

I am alone.

I shake myself. *He wouldn't hurt me. He isn't like the others.* My mind trips on the words. *From my time.*

In a moment, he returns. To my utter disbelief, he drops beside me, a rag in his hand. I shake my head, my lips working through silent, amazed words as he sops up the horrid mess I've made.

His eyes are anxious as they flick up. "You *must* lie down. I understand about your brother. I know you're frantic, but you're not fit to walk…let alone walk through time." The last words are strained, his face disbelieving.

"Oh John, John." My lips tremble. Panic squeezes my brain, arriving in the center of a dense, mental fog. I picture a long hallway. I feel, and know, behind each door be the gaping maw of death.

I have only to choose which way to die. John, as a wee boy, walks down the hall. My mind flashes again.

John's tiny two-year-old hands, reaching up to me, to lift him off a dirt floor.

His gapped-tooth-smile as he presents his first precocious drawing.

"Verity? Verity?" I hear his voice. It sounds far away.

He snaps his fingers in front of my eyes.

Suddenly, I am rising off the floor and I feel my

head against his chest. He places me on the bed with such care it fractures my heart. Surely I do not deserve such treatment.

I grasp his hand and squeeze. "*Please*, I must return. They will kill him-he will *hang*. I told you, everyone in Salem is either afflicted or accused."

The drive to move, to act, to leave this infernal, comfortable bed shakes my insides.

His hands stroke his concerned face, and he stands, pacing beside the bed. "I will go down to the corn and see if the door is open."

"You would?"

"Of course, as soon as I'm sure you're well."

"What time be this?"

"The twenty-first century."

I nod but it still feels too big an idea to fit inside my head.

I open my eyes and stare at my surroundings in a whole new way. Contraptions abound, the likes of which I've never imagined, let alone seen. How odd, to see creations for which I have no name. I feel like Adam.

"This year is black."

"Excuse me?" He stops pacing and his blue eyes instantly flick to my face, intense.

"Nothing."

He quickly drops beside me on the bed. His hand cradles mine, and the warmth of it cuts through the panic, quieting the antics of my heart. My headache is easing.

The hornets howl; they do not like him. His mere presence dulls them to a low hum.

"No, it's all right. You don't have to be afraid

with me. I won't let anyone or anything harm you."

His sincere eyes make me want to blurt out every secret I've ever kept. My traitorous breath hitches again. I close my eyes, too cowardly to watch his judgment.

"I am…different." I peek up to evaluate his expression.

"You've come to the right place, then."

My eyebrow rises with the question forming on my lips. "T-Truman?"

"Please, don't act so hesitant. I've already admitted I can't keep my mind off you. Pathetically so. I'm different, too."

His face turns rapturous—like I've given him with the most perfect gift he's ever seen.

"I, I—" he stutters. His eyes cloud with his own protective sheen. He winces. "People emit colors for me, and their names have tastes, for that matter. You, for instance...are now the most beautiful shade of purple."

I lean over, looking past him to a looking glass. My own quizzical expression stares back. His gaze follows mine, and his face flushes.

"No, only *I* can see it. It seems to be tied to people's personalities. Almost like…an anchor to their souls? Who they *really* are?"

"Oh," I breathe. "Really?" *How could he know these things? My mind asks a question, I don't want answered. Could he be in league with the dark one?*

His expression shifts back to concern. "I can feel your fear, right now. I swear, it's scientific, nothing supernatural. You're outlined in red, around the purple now. And the squint of your eyes, the doubtful slant of your mouth…well they scream fear. I am positive."

"Supernatural?"

"I'm not a witch or anything. Also, I can just look at people's expressions, and decipher them—tell when they're lying. It's automatic."

"Oh, all right. I…" I hesitate. I have never admitted my abnormality to another, save my family. "See days, months, letters—in color."

"Yes! I've studied it! Color-grapheme synesthesia. Why that's the most common kind. The statistics say one in every two-hundred people have a form of it."

"What? It has a name? Other people have it too?"

"Most definitely. I find it fascinating."

Tears of relief spring up and trail down my cheeks. A reluctant hope clogs my heart, making it skip a beat.

"They all proclaimed me a witch. They would've *killed me.* And you say it be…normal?"

"For you, yes."

Anger consumes hope. I grasp a handful of my hair and shake it at him. "And the way I look? My eyes, do you have the answer for them, as well?"

"It has a big name, too. Heterochromia. But also normal—for you. I can show pictures of others on the internet."

"The w-what?"

Sobs break the encrusted façade around my heart. Years of silence, of suppressing every fear, every thought—relief busts it open, shattering in my chest.

His warm, muscled arms pull me into his embrace. I try to lose myself in his scent. Try not to think. He smells so clean, compared to other men.

But I've never been this close before, to anyone.

My voice is muffled into his shirt. "You said people's names have tastes. What do I taste like?" I lift my eyes to take in his face, embarrassment heating my cheeks.

His cheeks redden in return. I almost laugh.

Dueling embarrassments.

"Like the snow. Pure and precise and…invigorating." A smile parts his lips. I feel the unfamiliar longing inside me. His eyes widen slightly as if he senses it, and he pulls me tighter in his arms.

He slowly bends his head toward me and his lips graze mine-softly at first, then they move furiously, with crushing swipes.

I open my mouth and close my eyes, savoring the feeling. A hot flush rushes up my neck and I grasp the back of his hair in both my hands.

I must not. I must not.

But I cannot stop. I've waited so long...to have something to love.

He pulls back abruptly, his face suddenly serious with some unspoken realization.

"I will help you get back to Salem. To find your brother, but only if I can come with you."

* * *

John jerked awake. Something had passed over his leg. He shivered.

I shall not look.

His mind paraded an endless stream of pictures. Pictures of comfort—his talisman against the continuous, almost inhuman, moans of the accused.

He'd found a piece of shale within reach of his bars. So far, one half of his coffin cell was scrawled in memories.

One wall housed his boyhood home, the sprawling countryside in Maine, where life was happy, before his parents' death. He barely remembered it now; just random images, conjured from the back of his mind.

On the other side, he sketched a quiet pond near the Parris household. He and Verity's secret meeting place.

"John, son. It's time to go. Your trial be today."

Constable Corwin opened the cell. John's legs quivered as he tried to stand. He clutched uselessly at the bars as they buckled. Corwin and the boy caught him beneath his arms, dragging him toward the light.

Pangs of searing pain shot through his thighs with each step.

"Open the door!" Corwin called into the other room.

As they entered the Ordinary, and the makeshift courtroom, he felt the heat of a hundred eyes judging him. A shudder, borne of their scorn, slid down his spine.

His eyes slid across their faces and he sucked in the musty air, trying to fill his lungs.

His mind screamed retreat, to pull inside, like a turtle to its shell.

But inside, Verity's voice warned, "You must defend yourself John. Show no fear."

A choked sob escaped, nonetheless.

Hands seated him roughly on a bench, where the accused were queued in the order of their hearings. Judge Hathorne pounded his gavel for attention.

"Candy, slave of Mrs. Hawkes. You are hereby accused of witchcraft. How do you plead?"

"Candy no witch in her country. Candy's mother no witch. Candy no witch Barbados. This country, mistress, give Candy witch."**

"So your mistress made you a witch in this country?"

"Yes, Mistress bring Candy ink, book and make Candy sign." The woman pretended to scribble an imaginary pen.

"Your spectral self is accused of attacking Mary Walcott and Anne Putnam, Jr."

John scoffed to the woman beside him, "Is there any afflicted who has *not* attacked Anne?"

Constable Corwin shot him a glare, and he pressed his lips together.

"How did you afflict these women?" Hathorne prompted.

"If Candy allowed, she will fetch the items."

Candy left the courtroom, flanked on either side by two men. Within minutes, she returned with an armful of belongings. In one hand was a handkerchief, which circled a piece of cheese and a piece of grass and was knotted in the middle. And in the other, she grasped two knotted rags.

Her feet no more than crossed the threshold when Mary Warren and Abigail and Deliverance Hobbs dropped to the ground, their bodies convulsing. The sound of Deliverance's head bouncing up and down off the floor reminded John of smashing pumpkins.

Mary's eyes filled with terror as they locked with Candy's. "She and her mistress and the man in black, they pinch us with the rags!"

Judge Hathorne screamed, “Remove those from her immediately.” His gaze never left the spectacle of the women, who now shuddered and flipped like suffocating fishes.

Removing the items from Candy produced no relief. Abigail Hobbs screamed in pain and grasped her leg as if bitten.

Hawthorne intervened once again. “Untie the knots; they must be the voodoo items. A knot for each of their souls.”

Corwin hurried over and untied the knots, looking expectantly at the writhing trio.

“No good, sir,” Corwin said.

Deliverance screamed, “Mercy, please sir!” Her head twisted and angled to the right as if slapped.

“Candy, eat the grass!” he commanded.

Candy looked as mortified as the witnesses. She shuffled over and stuffed the piece of grass into her mouth. She chewed it quickly and opened her mouth, like a child, to show she had swallowed it.

Mary’s fit reached apoplectic proportions. Her form went tombstone-rigid, and her eyes rolling back to show the whites.

John could scarcely breathe. The only time he’d seen such violent fits was when his father had shot a dog infected with the distemper.

His desperate mind yearned for Verity, and he imagined her steadying hand on his shoulder. He felt vibration in his throat and realized he was moaning.

Hathorne screamed, “Burn the rags, Corwin!”

Constable Corwin hurried outside and returned, brandishing a foot warmer. He shoved one of the rags inside and quickly lit it. The dry piece of fabric blazed orange in the center of the dusky room.

Every soul held its breath. Would the rag's destruction halt the chaos?

Deliverance's wail fractured the silence. Her hands patted all over her chest, as if extinguishing flames. "It burns us! AHHHHH!"

Hathorne's face was now visibly flushed despite the dim light. "Douse it man!"

Corwin bolted outside, returning with a bucketful of water. Half of it sloshed on the floor as he skidded to a stop in front of the burning heap.

As the arc of water poured onto the flame, strangled choking sounds emitted from all three women.

Abigail managed a whisper. "You be drowning us!"

John's hands flew to his eyes. He slipped into his head, reveling in the pictures there, willing his soul to *be* there.

The room faded to a distorted reality, as if underwater. He knew his eyes were unfocused and far away. Verity had begged him to never escape, described how his face frightened her when he escaped. "Like a house abandoned," she'd whispered.

He cared not.

Finally, a woman stood across the room, her hand clutching at her heart. Mrs. Hawkes was barely heard over the din of the hapless trio on the floor. "I confess, Candy and I are guilty."

The women's writhing halted immediately and they lay still as the stones on the floor.

In a far off voice, he heard Hathorne say, "Return the other prisoners. This is enough devilry for one day."

John felt hands grasp both his arms.

He did not struggle as they hauled him back toward the witch-dungeon.

***Author's Note: part of dialogue was from actual Salem transcripts.*

Chapter 15

I rub the soft dress betwixt my fingers, wondering at its texture. I gaze at the young woman in the full-length mirror; unconvinced it is truly my face which stares back.

Sunshine peers over my shoulder, watching me with a tender expression. She smooths my shoulders and steps back. "Well, it seems to fit well. Will that be okay?"

The dress is charcoal gray and I fidget as I try in vain to pull it down. My knees poke out the bottom, making me self-conscious.

At home, to show one's *ankles* be scandalous. The top bodice is tight and gathered, culminating in what they call a 'turtleneck'. My dark red ringlets are a bright contrast lying against it. Sunshine has completed my *'make-up'* as she calls it, and one eyebrow rises in evaluation. She nods, admiring her handiwork.

"I never had a little sister," she quips, arranging my hair behind me.

The result is remarkable. I pivot from side to side, trying to reassure myself I am *truly* the reflection. I look as beautiful as any of the gentry back home. If I wore a ball gown, I would be indistinguishable from the classes I've served.

"Well, say something. Your eyes look fantastic with that color of eye shadow. They totally pop."

I blink and look closer. "That shadowing makes their unevenness more pronounced. Are you certain it's acceptable? I don't want to attract too much attention."

Sunshine pops a hand to her hip. "Honey, that's impossible. You were breathtaking covered in mud. And your eye color is cool. I've seen actresses with two different eye colors, but never met anyone in person. They're beautiful and different."

I blink again, one dark brown and one blue-green eye stare back at me. I bite my lip and meet her gaze.

"Where I'm from…calling attention to yourself, *standing out*, is a sin."

Sunshine laughs. "Well, we got a whole world of sinners now then!"

Shame burns my face, and I curse my eyes for wetting as Sunshine's smile falters.

"I'm sorry. I know this is all totally foreign and awful for you. It will be fine—no one will stone you or anything for the way you look, okay? I promise."

I don't trust my voice, so I nod and feign a smile.

"Besides, Truman would most likely rip their heads off if they got near you."

A hot blush creeps up my turtleneck.

Sunshine doesn't notice and motions for me to follow.

"So, we've told the children you're an O.T. student, who is visiting from a local university. You remember what that is, right?"

"Yes, an occupational therapist. Someone who

treats many different types of physical and mental illnesses, correct?"

Over the past few weeks, Sunshine and Truman have pummeled me with instructions on how to behave. Truman tried the time door several times, but it will not open. Now that I can wander under the guise of a student, I will haunt the door every hour till it permits me entry.

"Yes! You have a fantastic memory, also like Truman. The man's a walking encyclopedia. He scares me, really." She chuckles, but it's an uncomfortable sound. "I think he even tones it down around me so I don't feel totally intimidated."

"Yes, remember the color-word marriages," I remind her. I tap my temple. "That aids my memory."

"Right! Synesthesia. You two are a little too alike if you ask me. Like you were plucked from the same mold, but landed in two different…times." She shakes her head, disbelief still coloring her features.

I tug at the hemline. "The dress is lovely, Sunshine. But I feel naked with my knees showing."

"Oh, honey. Wait till you see what is on television now. I'll keep some smelling salts handy."

I follow Sunny down the stairs.

Truman is standing at the entrance to the O.T. clinic, waiting. All the children are off to school, and the quiet of the house is deafening from the previous two hours of organized chaos.

As we step into the light, a little whistle escapes his lips.

Apparently unintentional, as he quickly runs his hand through his hair.

His stare is intense and raises the hairs on my

neck.

I drop my eyes to the floor. He reminds me of a tentative groom seeing his bride for the first time.

I shiver. A jolt of electricity flashed from my heart to my stomach.

It's unwise to allow him such power.

I know it. But I cannot stop it.

I pray he is exactly as he appears. He seems too good to be true. I smile at my pun.

"Wow. I barely recognized you. Except for your color—it's vibrant purple now, love."

My breath sucks in at his smile and his eyes dance.

I shift, self-conscious again. "It is acceptable, then?"

He laughs, grasping my hand.

Leaning in close to my face, he whispers, "That's a poor choice of words. It's like saying the Mona Lisa is *acceptable*."

Sunshine clears her throat.

Truman's eyes do not leave mine. "She looks great, Sunny. Your charts are in room two. See you at lunch." He waves her away.

Sunshine snorts as her boots stomp into the other room.

Truman checks his pocket watch, and then leans in, dangerously close. I smell his sweet breath and a little shudder courses down my back as the longing roars.

I realize the hornets are absent. I haven't heard their buzzing for days. I'm relieved, but the fear creeps around, looking for a way back in.

I know they will return the moment I'm alone.

Truman closes the small gap between us and all else fades. Only the tickle of his breath on my lips.

"May I kiss you?"

I swallow. "Yes."

His thin lips are soft as they graze mine and his breath intakes sharply.

His hand slides into my hair, grasping the base of my neck as the stroking of his lips intensifies. Our lips move with perfect, heated synchrony for a few seconds. It's like dancing.

The hornets resume, squalling in my ear till the vibration rocks my head. I pull back.

"Verity?"

My voice is breathless. "It just makes me nervous. Where I come from, you can spend a day in the stocks for public affection. And they're torture. I know."

I reflexively rub my wrists, where the ghosts of the manacles remain.

"After we find John, and we will…." Truman trails off.

My gaze drops to the floor with the mention of my brother.

My heart beats in irregular patterns as if mangled. I miss him so much it's unbearable.

Truman's finger slides gently beneath my chin, raising it; forcing me to look him in the eye.

"I want the two of you to consider staying. Here. With me. *Please*."

A tremble ripples in my heart. In what *fashion* would he have me stay?

"Forgive me, Truman. Your kindness is beyond comprehension. But might I ask in what capacity? Perhaps John and I could be your domestics?"

The curtsey happens without thought. I blush, feeling ridiculous—but it's ingrained in me.

My confusion buzzes with the hornets; I will assume nothing. Assumptions are dangerous.

Truman's lips tremble and he roars with laughter.

"What is so funny, good sir?" I ask indignantly.

He forces the grin away. "Nothing. Of course we'll find jobs for you and John. But I truly hope you and I can be more than…*employer and employee.* I don't normally kiss my employees."

"Praise be for small miracles!" Sunshine's voice calls from the other room.

Truman yells back, "Shut it. Aren't I paying you to work? Or something?"

The front door knob twists, ending our conversation. A harried-looking woman kicks it open, holding her boy at the wrist. The boy flops to the ground, wailing and spitting.

Truman turns and says quietly enough so only I may hear. "So it begins.

* * *

John plugged his ears, but the conversation was too close to block. The arguing couple's cell was right next to his own.

Martha and Giles Corey voices rose loudly enough for the whole of the dungeon to hear.

"How could you accuse me, Giles? Me, your own wife, of witchcraft?"

John listened intently. Giles Corey was known as a man who never minced words, and had a countenance only the devil could love.

He winced, thinking of a barely-thwarted thrashing for accidentally tripping Corey on the street. It was rumored he'd once caned the village idiot to death.

"I was mistaken. You are no more a witch than I," Giles says.

"What are we to do now? Both of our sons-in-law are siding against us? What of a petition on our behalf?"

Giles spits. "That is what I think of petitions. Many signatures have been drafted on behalf of the accused—old Rebecca Nurse, John and Elizabeth Proctor, Mary Bradbury, it did not a whit of good. The names not worth the paper they were writ upon. And who will come to my defense? You, yourself, called me a devilish rogue!"

Martha sobbed into her hands.

"I have a notion, Mary. You shall see." Corey placed his hands on the bars, speaking to all in the dungeon. "I refuse to confess to a crime of which I am innocent. You know full-well, they will take our belongings if I do. We will go free, but a lifetime of work-stolen unjustly. *I will not have it!*" he roared. His voice echoed through the cells.

Martha's weeping incited an entire chorus of women and their wails combined in an eerie echo.

John covered his ears. The sound was God's hammer, splitting his skull.

"Look at these wretches. Even if they're pronounced innocent, they will remain jailed for their inability to pay. And stay here till they rot."

His old, bony finger shot-out accusingly at John. "Like you, artist-boy. Your soul be doomed."

Chapter 16

I crouch in the corner of the room Truman calls the O.T. Clinic. He's trying to coax the little wild boy into a chair.

I flinch and the boy dodges, ready to run if he charges me. His little teeth have already left one raging-red, bite-mark on Truman's forearm.

I must be fair. My brother is different, but John was never violent. I swallow.

"Verity, it's okay. He's just a boy, really. A boy no one understands—but underneath it all, just a child. I call them Lost Boys."

"Lost Boys?"

"Yes, Peter Pan? Wait, that may have been after your time."

The boy's eyes, perceptive and aware, see Truman's attention has left him.

He bolts, reaching a swing that's bolted to the ceiling and launches onto it, belly down and spread-eagled, flying into the air.

My hands fly to cover my mouth.

"No-you-don't!" To my surprise, Truman laughs. A low chuckle that somehow manages to sound sad.

He runs across the room, catching the boy up into his arms. The boy relents, letting Truman wrestle him into a chair.

Truman holds up a toy, *Thomas the Tank Engine*, he calls it, in front of the boy's face. His little eyes widen and sharpen. A moment prior, they were dim and unfocused—but now, they're *clear*. It's like watching the breeze blow away storm clouds.

The change is astounding. I hold my breath.

"P-please," the boy says, concurrently rubbing his chest in a circle.

Truman claps. He turns to me and translates his joy. "That movement on his chest is the sign for *please* as well! A double success! It's very difficult for him to communicate, or control himself," he says, indifferently pointing to the angry bite on his arm.

Truman lays three numbers on the ground, placing the Thomas Engine on the third.

On the number one, he places some stringing beads, and on the number two, some picture cards.

"First this," he says, pointing, "and then that." He finishes by pointing to the train, an obvious reward for the boy's enduring the first two tasks.

The boy's face screws up into a quivering ball of fury.

A defiant, high-pitched screech rips through the air.

I cover my ears and shrink back. *It's like taming wild animals.*

The boy bolts toward the swing, again.

Truman picks up his walkie-talkie, still shadowing the boys every movement. "Sunshine, what day of the week is November 23rd?"

"It's a Saturday, Truman." The words are out before I can stop them.

His head whips toward me, mouth agape. He quickly faces the boy again, who is now scaling a ladder, intent on using the slide to take flight.

Sunshine's voice crackles back, "It's a Saturday, Truman."

His eyes narrow. "Are you able to do that, then? Visualize the whole calendar?"

I bite my lip and nod. Another secret, confessed. The months and years of the calendar flip through my head, a kaleidoscope of color.

"It's also a purple day."

I smile, but the sides of my mouth are trembling.

I am terrified one of these revelations will make him turn on me.

I want, more than anything else in the world, for this man to accept me. No, *love me*. Make me his own.

In every way possible.

But he smiles, and another bit of my soul heals.

"I had a patient who could do that. A young man with Asperger's syndrome."

"What is that?"

"In a bit, let me get Adam on his way first."

A half hour passes quickly. Truman expertly coaxes the boy through his tasks, identifying pictures through pointing.

He explains, "The pictures help him to communicate the thoughts trapped in his head."

The child manages a few words, here and there. Truman wrestles him through an odd whirlwind of activities—bouncing on a ball, and swinging the boy through the air while he whoops in delight.

He calls the combined tasks a *sensory diet*, explaining the boy's senses are immature.

Finally, his mother appears and he tantrums—*again.*

"Honestly Adam, first I can't get you in here, and now I can't get you out!"

Truman's smile is sage. "Yes, I call that the *'I hate it, do it again'*.

Truman is quiet till he hears the outside door click shut.

His eyes are immediately on me, *all me*.

I'm amazed how calm he is, after an hour of screams. *My* nerves feel flayed and raw.

"I believe Asperger's is a way of being, not necessarily a disorder. Some disagree, and say it's on the autism spectrum. It's a genetic occurrence."

"That's what you said Adam has?"

"Yes. Well, he's got P.D.D., but people with Asperger's aren't good with other people, and can be highly intelligent. I bet half of NASA has Aspergers."

"What's NASA?"

"Never mind. They also tend to have limited interests, but can talk your ear off about whatever excites them!"

He laughs, again. It has a warm, musical sound, like a cello.

"That sounds like John. He will speak about his paintings for hours on end, but can't be bothered with people he doesn't know." Tears spring immediately on my lower lids.

I miss him so desperately. Every thought of him punches a ragged, gaping hole in my chest.

And the constant, nagging fear for his life has resurrected the hornets, giving them an endless buzzing symphony.

Even Truman's comforting presence barely keeps them at bay.

I swallow. Truman is watching me. He is the most perceptive man I've ever met. He takes my hand in his.

"He's a magnificent artist, and that's his only love, besides me. And he constantly misreads words and intentions, or what people's faces say about the way they feel. He is doomed without me. I *must* get back to him."

I close my eyes. My hands are shaking.

I smell Truman move closer, sliding his arm about my shoulders. "Go out and check the door as many times as you like, love. I'll be in here, doing more of this, all day long. Come and get me if it's open. I…" he hesitates. "Take the walkie-talkie with you."

I open my eyes. I know by the stretched tone of his voice, he's about to say something important.

His lips press together in a tight line. He thrusts the walkie-talkie into my hand.

His strong, wiry arms hug me fiercely. He presses his forehead against the side of my head.

The desperation seeps into his voice. "I don't want to lose you. I want to come with you to save your brother."

I pull back, scrutinizing his expression. "What if you can't get back through?"

His eyes narrow and seem to take a deep breath of their own.

"I've been alone most of my life. I wasn't adopted till fourteen, and let's just say I have *attachment* issues." He swallows; his prominent Adam's apple bobs. "I'm wholly attached to you-and I've only just met you. You know more about me than anyone alive. There is so much I want to know about you. *I want to know everything.* I want to be able to finish your sentences. Help you walk when you're old. Home is in your heart, Verity; so that is wherever *you are*. Whether in my century, or yours."

My heart is a wild, fluttering bird. "You *love* me?"

He smiles widely. "I do."

A rapturous joy bubbles forth. But danger lies beneath it.

To dare to *hope.* But that's all we need, really.

The hornets quiet. *Perhaps they die.*

I fling my arms around his neck. A singular tear slides down my cheek, dropping onto his chest.

I feel dizzy. I want time to halt. To stay suspended in this perfect moment.

"I feel the same."

Sunshine's voice crackles into the clinic through the walkie-talkie. The button was depressed, where I'm leaning on it. She heard everything.

"I hate to interrupt the 90210 episode, but your next patient is here."

* * *

John's hands' shook. Mercifully, someone had provided a sketchbook, perhaps selfishly hoping he would draw and record the courtroom scene.

This could not be further from his mind. He unearthed his favorite memories of comfort. A page-by-page account of his peaceful life with Verity, and the dog they'd had before their parent's death. His fingers twitched, reliving the feel of his shiny, black fur.

His fingers scrambled across the page, shading and contouring Verity's face as she sat rocking by the blazing fire. The huge, black dog draped across her feet.

The hot sting of tears came again, but he paid them no mind. They made a tapping sound on the parchment.

He'd given up, giving them free reign. His feelings spun out, unrelenting, like a child's top.

The colors in his head grew with his exhaustion.

He was so weary.

Tired of fear, tired of pain, and oh so tired of speaking.

The slightest movements caused long streaks of iridescent lights to slash across his vision.

Sleep was impossible in the coffin cell. His long legs jutted out the bars and he often woke to the scratching claws of rats.

His days were *plagued* with lightning fast, dizzying colors from the lack of sleep. He only heard fractions of what was said to him.

The world was too bright, people's voices, too loud.

The inside of his mind was preferable. It was becoming more and more difficult to translate the constant stream of pictures in his mind into words. Like he was slipping away.

And emotions…trying to describe them left him standing at a bright green hill, words lodged half-way between his mind and his mouth. Like being trapped in your own head.

"How do you plead, Mr. Corey?"

Judge Hathorne, nicknamed *the hanging judge*, stared unflinchingly into Corey's anguished face.

John's eyes jumped up and down the defendant's queued the bench beside him. He was number six once again. Most likely, his trial would be delayed. He secretly felt it the hand of God at work, postponing his trial, till Verity returned to his rescue.

Giles Corey stood mute once again. The old man shuffled his feet, but remained silent. His lips crammed together over his crooked black teeth.

His friend, Thomas Gardner, spoke out of turn. "Giles, enter a plea, save your soul and confess! Please, man!"

"That will be enough, Mr. Gardener. Unless you'd like to be escorted outside," Hathorne scolded.

A woman whispered beside him, "If he won't enter a plea, they cannot take his land."

John's head swiveled as Hathorne's booming voice resumed.

"You leave me no choice, Mr. Corey. Death by pressing."

The world seemed to spiral away. His next coherent thought was the sound of screams, forcing him out of his blissful oblivion.

Martha Corey's frantic wails echoed through the ordinary. One hand rose futilely as they ushered Giles out the door.

His death march. For what?

John stood, peering out the window. Quickly he turned his head and closed his eyes as his mind shuddered.

Too late. The imprint of the scene burned

indelibly on his memory.

He forced himself to watch. His teeth chattered in his head.

Mr. Corey lay face-up in the open pastureland across the street from the jail; while a morbid group of spectators looked on.

John's view was limited, and he was grateful.

Constable Corwin placed flat boards across the older man's chest. Other men heaped massive stones on top. John silently thanked God Mrs. Corey had no window near her.

The pressing lasted for two days, long after they'd re-entered the witch dungeon.

The sounds of the pressing echoed through the dungeon.

After one full day of screaming, Mrs. Corey crumpled and lay silent. Motionless on the bottom of her cell.

When the guards returned, he overheard them talking.

Corey could've stopped the pressing with a word, a plea of guilty or no.

Instead, the only words he whispered were, "More weight."

Chapter 17

Verity

The afternoon sun is hot against my back. I glance down at the corn-maze map to be sure I'm on the correct path.

The rows are well worn and mud inches its way up my boots, almost up to my laces.

I tilt my head, listening for the music. It's been absent for days now.

The corn rustles and my heart leaps to my throat.

I spin, listening, waiting.

A bright flash of blue erupts as a flock of bluebirds alight from all around me. *They followed me.*

I walk faster, eyes darting everywhere. I believe many oddities to live in the corn. Lurking and watching my progress.

The corn is withering and I think of the voices, wandering somewhere, perhaps as close as the wind in my ear.

I picture them; a funnel cloud of sounds, ripping up the rows. Gooseflesh sprints up my arms, raising my hairs.

How can this place be in so many times at once? Is it the divine justice of a Creator? To somehow right the wrongs of history?

A song begins a few rows over. Gooseflesh prickles my arms.

I flinch, but keep walking forward, clutching the walkie-talkie tighter.

It is the same serenade that emanates from the whirlwind. I shake my head. Nothing shall keep me from John.

After searching for a quarter hour, the bridge appears.

It is Wednesday, the blue day. The door has always opened on Tuesdays—Tuesdays are red. It is also the day that marks my parents' deaths.

I wonder if that is why my mind inked it indelible red?

My stifled panic breaks loose, strangling my chest. Like long-buried lungs, taking their resurrection gasp.

Being with Truman kept it at bay—without his calming presence, it smothers me, inching up my throat.

And of course, *my friends* buzz to life.

I spit on the ground, furious they've returned to haunt my ears.

I've made it to the bridge. Behind me, I hear the whispers, the bluebirds and the rainbow-song serenade calling. Growing louder and louder with every step.

I sprint up the bridge, hurling myself across the apex.

For a brief second, whilst I'm air born, I'm bittersweet.

I will see John.

Then my boots strike the bridge. I look up to see

the same, brooding Pennsylvania sky.

"No! No!"

I glower at the heavens.

"Why is this happening? John needs me. You must open."

Tears seep out and rage flushes my face.

"I know you hear me!" I bellow at the stalks. "You see all that happens in this field! Show yourselves, unless you be cowards."

I press my hands to my forehead.

A cheerless tune saturates the corn, and with it, a deluge of images in my mind's eye.

My fingers rush to the gun Truman insisted I carry.

The music drowns my senses as the doleful, orchestral piece unravels inside me. The music digs beneath my buried memories, popping them to the forefront.

My mother and father lie on the floor of the cabin, their corpses newly pale, waxen.

I choke, my fingers claw my face.

They've been bled out, like animals.

Each is face down in a hideous, crimson circle.

My teeth chatter, rattling my skull.

"It's over. It's all over now. Just a memory."

My hands cradle my head, as I try to keep the fragments of my skull, *my soul*, together.

Righteous anger burns out the images.

I square my shoulders, looking for my tormentor.

This is not helping.

Verity. It is my mother's voice. Strong and earnest. *You must live. Save your brother.*

The images rear again, a monster refusing to die.

My brother, toddling in a circle, his eyes wide with fear; around him, cruel children taunt, "Idiot! Idiot!"

I ball my dress in my shaking hands.

My mother's voice shouts, silencing the hornets. Love is their poison.

John needs you. Be strong. Save him. You have not time to be frightened.

I hear them, then. The whispers on the wind.

My head swivels left and right. Bits of conversations swirl, popping in and out around me in a circle.

Like several personalities are debating, examining me.

She needs us.

Why her?

She is chosen.

"I want to go home. My brother needs me."

The words grow louder, arguing in a heated whisper, till the air is clogged with raspy, verbal spider-webs.

"He will die!" I plead. "Please."

My legs give way. Pain shoots through my knees as they strike the wooden bridge.

The whispers intensify, till I can hear and see the tiny funnel cloud generated by their arguments.

It encircles a cornstalk, spiraling up and down, faster and faster, spitting out yellow kernels.

They sink into the ground, disappearing.

A twisted vine erupts from the dirt and climbs; two-four-six feet, in the space of a breath.

It splinters with a thunderclap, in a myriad of directions, like woody capillaries. Its writhing tendrils scrawl to form words.

My heart hammers. They are alive?

The brown-briar spirals, weaving in and on itself. The length of it expands and contracts, as if breathing. It stretches and grows till a reedy tapestry spans ten feet across.

It stops, and I wait in a loud silence.

Even the bluebirds, perched on top of every stock, are silent.

At first, I see nothing.

I squint my eyes and cock my head as the patterns slowly appear.

I walk off the bridge.

Words appear at an alarming rate, the vines twisting, curling, and stretching to accommodate the script.

"Face your fears."

My fears are mind-shattering. I do not wish to *acknowledge* them, let alone face them.

I hold out my hand, feeling for the murmuring breeze, but it's gone.

The air turns tight and caustic. I choke on it, and cry out as I look up.

A discolored field of wheat appears, its blackened heads bending in the breeze.

A forest materializes in a blink, in the middle of the cornfield.

Every branch is covered in them, like macabre, hanging decorations.

They're endless in number, as far as my eye can see. They materialize in and out with every breath of the breeze.

Nooses swing from every limb.

* * *

John's body shook.

It began with a finger twitch. It traveled like a lightning-strike up his arm and he was its pawn.

His boot banged rapid-fire off the wood floor.

His thigh screamed; the contraction spread like an invisible vice, milking his legs, contorting his torso. His arms jerked straight like a scarecrow.

The muscles seized in a collective-clench and he toppled from the bench. Like a petrified boy.

The seizure changed its mind. His limbs rippled without purpose; his head crashed and bounced off the ordinary floor.

"Someone help John!" A young woman's voice called beside him. "John, who be afflicting you? Help us help you," she pleaded.

No-one *did this* to him. He was not enchanted, he was ill. Just like that poor dog after eating the witch-cake.

The twitching began last night directly after he ate the bread.

"No one t-t-torments me, I am ill."

Finally, the contractions released him.

He lay still, waiting; every few seconds his limbs gave a residual twitch.

His head felt empty and numb, and he welcomed it; the corners of his mind were mercifully quiet.

His body was hauled to sitting; his head lolling to the side.

The same girl's voice spoke up. Her voice sounded far away. "Surely his trial should be stayed."

A male voice responded, "We have put his

judgment off too many times already. Begin."

Constable Corwin's voice was so close, he felt his breath on his ear. "John, please recite the Lord's Prayer."

John licked his cracked lips, and was thankful when a tear wet the hardened skin.

"Our Father, who art in heaven, hallowed be thy n-name."

"Continue."

"Thy kingdom c-c-c-c-c-c-c-c-," another seizure shook him, shaking his voice out of control. His leg banged against the desk and he howled in pain.

Across the room, a chorus of screams echoed in the ordinary.

John forced his eyes open to see the familiar pack of girls, writhing and contorting in response to his stutter.

He stared, beseeching Hathorne. "I cannot help it."

All three girls mimicked in sing-song voices. "I cannot help it."

"Stop!" John yelled.

"Stop!" They chanted.

"Condemned. He is a witch. Unable to state the Lord's prayer, a sure sign of guilt. Date to be set for hanging. Remove him, please."

John couldn't speak.

He prayed. Someone must save him.

Chapter 18

The voices follow me. I'm running, dodging them, dodging the stocks. One slashes my cheek, but I don't miss a step.

The orphanage roof is visible. I'm almost there.

A deafening flutter hits my ears. The bluebirds are giving chase.

I glance back, stumble and look forward again; afraid the voices will catch me.

As one, they leave the path and fly above the corn-tops. The squawks and shrieks are deafening. They've grown in number; they're uncountable. The flock folds in and on itself, reminding me of the ocean's tumbling surf.

I break out the corn's mouth and the congregation halts, fluttering about the entrance. As if they are bound to the corn.

Only here. In Salem, they go where they please.

"They *do* travel through the doors."

My heart is in my mouth and I bolt for the house.

The worry is a part of me now, like an arm or leg and the hornets feast on my anxiety.

I stand on the porch, trying to catch my breath.

The bluebirds are slowly leaving, and I can't hear the voices. They are trapped in the corn as well.

The tears on my cheeks are almost dry, but I swipe them again. No sense upsetting the children, they have their own worries.

I open the front door. Raised voices filter from the kitchen. I turn the corner and hesitate, watching.

Ram and True have managed to get every boy at the table—more or less.

A few smaller children crawl under tables.

"We're losing the battle, I sense a mutiny," Truman says to Ram, grasping a four-year-old boy by the scruff and placing him back into his seat. "Eat."

Ram sees me first and nods to Truman; his eyes narrow and scrutinize his friend's expression.

Truman looks up from tying Anthony's shoe, and relief floods his face.

His half-smile constricts my chest.

He slides his chair back and his eyes never leave my face.

It's as if I'm the only person in the room.

My skin burns under his touch as his fingers grasp my elbow. He leads me into the hallway-away from ten sets of staring eyes.

A collective, "OOOO!" echoes down the hall.

"Zip it or no dessert!" Ram's chastises.

Truman leans in so close, his breath tickles my cheek.

He kisses it gently.

I lick my lips, which feel suddenly dry.

"I'm so thankful you're all right," he breathes quietly, "I was about to go to the corn—you were gone quite awhile. And it's getting dark. All I got was static on the talkie." He kisses me again, feather-light on my lips and pulls away.

He eyes tighten. "It wouldn't open, then?"

"I saw…." I close my eyes, trying to name it. "The cyclone of sounds. Of voices."

Truman's hands rub up and down my arms. His eyes scan my body as if checking for injuries. "Did it speak?"

I nod. "It said, face your fears."

Truman's face drains. His eyes widen in comprehension. "Of course. I was so stupid."

"What do you mean? Speak plainly."

"Never mind. I'm going with you. The townsfolk will capture you, put you on trial. I've been studying Salem—we'll talk tonight, okay? After the tribe's in bed."

"Yes, of course."

He takes my hand, leading me back into the fray with a reluctant glance.

I give Ram a tentative smile, which he returns.

"Hi Miss Ver-i-ty," Anthony says.

I ruffle his hair and sit beside Truman at the table.

* * *

Next morning

They were sequestered behind the barn. Away from the tribe of prying eyes which currently gawked from every window of the farmhouse.

The words privacy and orphanage were oxymorons. He should know.

"Is there ennythin else I need to know before we open the door?"

"Remember, you cannot touch me in anyway. It

will land you in the stocks. Remember you are a gentleman; they shall be more likely to heed your words if they think you wealthy. So, I am beneath you—don't show too much interest in me. Like you do." Her face flushed.

He smiled. "That is so ludicrous."

"Truman, it's vitally important—"

He silenced her, placing his index over her lips, stealing another kiss.

"Sorry. I know it's important. I'll play my part. It's just barking to think the most important person in my world is beneath me because she wasn't born to wealth."

Anxiety raised its head. It was becoming real. This wasn't a game.

He paced beside her, thinking out loud.

"So I am to buy your service from the Putnams."

"Yes. You obviously don't have the right currency. You will have to barter."

He slid his hand in his pocket and extracted his great-grandfather's watch.

"We'll start with this, and I'll bring more heirlooms, for insurance. We'll find John, and bring him back. Hopefully without anyone getting hurt."

"I'm worried. I'm dreaming of him every night, now."

"We'll try every day, Verity. Starting now. Let's go see if it is open."

He glanced back at the orphanage. He felt the guilt on his face and covered by rubbing his growing beard.

"I hope Ram will get on without me."

Verity gave his arm a shake. "True-this isn't your

battle. You do not have to come—everyone in that house depends on you."

Her mismatched eyes dropped to the ground.

He touched her chin, and was momentarily distracted by its softness.

He waited till she met his gaze. "And who can *you* depend on, love? Annethin that affects you, affects *me*. C'mon, we're losing daylight."

They headed north, to the top of the maze. And the bridge.

Chapter 19

After hours of trying, we finally relented and returned to the house.

Truman is gazing out at the corn, his hand resting on the porch railing.

I keep crying. I can't help it. John shall die.

The words keep repeating, a haunting mantra in my head.

"Why won't it open?"

Truman's face matches the anguish in my heart. "I don't know. If I did, we'd already be there."

We continue to try and weeks fly by. I am as sick and stick-like as the scarecrow in the corn. I cannot eat or sleep—to breathe in and out each day seems too much.

I stare out my window into the night and shiver, thankful the voices and birds are bound between the stalks.

My heart is sinking.

Is John still alive? Does the chronology of time runs equally between the two worlds? If so, he is doomed.

I sigh. Two boys bolt past my room, darting down the hall.

I foresee bruises, and hurry to the door.

"You can't catch me!" Anthony teases, sticking his tongue out at the older boy.

"You are so dead," Tim replies.

They dart back toward me. I turn sideways, lifting a leg to avoid a collision.

"Sorry!" Tim shoots over his shoulder. He doesn't miss a step.

At the end of the hall, two deep voices argue but drop when they hear my footsteps.

It's odd. I'm closer to one of them in age than Truman, but our minds couldn't be further apart.

I'm jealous of how long children are permitted to *stay children* in this time.

This reality bonds Truman and I together. We barely remember the safety of childhood.

I head into my room and collapse onto my bed, draping my arm across my eyes.

The intercom buzzes and Truman's voice pipes into my room. "Ram, Edward is freaking out. Can you help me get him into bed?"

I stare at the speaker, taking deep, ridiculous breaths.

It's technology, not enchantment.

"Yeah, sure." Ram's reply is tired.

I know he resents me and I cannot blame him. I've wrecked his plans, stealing Truman's direction.

I take more breaths, trying to block out the sounds.

Life here is a stark contrast to Salem, where children are seen and not heard.

I shudder, thinking of Edward's fate, were he born in Salem.

He reminds me of a younger John. His violent

tantrums and inability to speak would've at best landed him a life in shackles, at worst…hanged for witchcraft.

I swallow and block the images. It's the only way I can carry on.

One of my mother's favorite phrases pops into my head. From the Holy Writings, *'Expectation postponed, makes the heart sick.'*

Here, children can say what they think, and play till all hours.

The Putnam household seems like solitary confinement in contrast. I count them on my fingers; ten children from age eighteen to three.

I check my watch and bolt upright. It is time to bathe the toddlers.

With so many children, it's imperative to follow the schedule. And, I admit, the nightly routine gives me comfort.

In a few moments the little ones are playfully splashing one another, not a care on their beautiful, tiny faces.

I stare at the hot water trickling from the spigot. It feels almost sinful, the way I can bathe daily. I check my watch again. It's time to tutor the older boys.

"Time to get out."

"No!" Both whine in unison.

I hurry down the stairs to the kitchen.

"It's time to get started."

The boys obediently sit at the kitchen table, handing me their assignments.

My fingers trace their spelling words. Truman enters behind me, and I startle.

He smiles, raising an eyebrow at my skittishness.

He takes me by the elbow into the hall, out of the boy's earshot.

"Why so anxious, love?"

I shrug. "Habit. Thinking of Salem again."

I cannot allow myself to call it home. This is home now. "Reading was a legacy in my family. Mother taught me and then I, John. Most women are only taught to sew and mind children."

My gift highlights words in my memory. Reading is as natural as breathing for me, so my mother's job had been simple.

Anthony pokes his tiny blond head around the corner, staring into the hallway.

I stare at Truman's face. His eyes are red-rimmed, watering with fatigue. "I'll take him back up, True."

"Thank you. I'm going to get another cup of coffee. I'll trade you chores."

I hoist the boy onto my hip, and feel his downy soft curls brush against my shoulder.

On impulse, I bury my nose in Anthony's sweet-smelling locks. I reach his room, and tuck him under the covers.

His eyes are full of trust before they disappear beneath thick lashes.

He reminds me of….

My heart *aches* for John. I pray he lives. The urge to return is a compulsion, never leaving my thoughts. I have no break from it.

Anthony's mouth yawns into a perfect circle and I smile despite the pain.

He looks perfectly contented, as a child should. With a realization, I understand Ram's resentment.

This place, this house, has such a noble purpose,

and I will be ruining someone's dream if Truman leaves.

To provide children like Anthony, the childhood they so deserve.

That I never had.

Truman is standing in the doorway, as if my doubts have summoned him. His deep russet hair is a mess, and his blue- green eyes narrow. He's always evaluating.

"You look so tired."

Truman pads quietly to Anthony and pulls the covers up to his nose. Anthony's eyes pop open and shine with the well-known routine.

"Say your prayers. Goodnight."

I stand and follow him to the doorway, where he flicks on a contraption called a night-light. He extinguishes the overhead light.

I fight the urge to switch it on and off, like one of the children.

"Sleep well. You know where to find me if ya' need me."

"Can I have the dog?"

"Sure. Pip!" He whistles.

The Border collie bounds into the room and follows his outstretched finger, snuggling against the boy.

He closes the door with a click.

He turns to face me, and I flinch.

His eyes are burning. They rove over me with an outright hunger.

I've seen that look before—mostly from drunks at the Ordinary. It used to frighten me.

But with him….

He doesn't speak.

The house sounds fade to nothing. The hornets, for this blissful moment, seem like someone else's nightmare.

His thumb caresses my hand with smoldering little circles. I swallow, watching his face.

A longing ripples down to my core.

He pushes me against the wall, leaning in, inches away.

It makes me nervous and I fiddle with the top of my shirt.

He noticed and grasps my hand. "It's only me. Doan be nervous. You're always safe with me."

He takes my hand and pulls me into his room.

I am vexed and my face surely says so.

He rolls his eyes playfully and pats the place beside him. I tentatively obey.

My heart pounds in my ears as he leans in, and his lips pet mine. His hands slide to my back, tracing the curve of my hip.

I sigh, which comes out like a shudder.

His scent, a mixture of strong soap and musk overwhelms me. He gathers a handful of my hair, placing it behind my shoulder.

Melancholy arrives, constricting my chest. Our time together may end—and it's been the best of my life.

I cannot be silent, I must leave him with no regrets.

"I'm so frightened we, this, will end when we return to Salem—I—"

He quiets my protests with a kiss. As the intensity escalates our mouths open and close and he presses the back of my head with his hand.

I hear my breathing—quick little gasps—in time with his fervent kisses. His tongue sweeps mine with a rising need.

Then his lips are gone. I open my eyes, confused. And longing. I am dizzy and disoriented.

His hands linger on the back of my head, as if he's reluctant to release me. His thick fingers toy with one of my red ringlets.

Ram passes by in the hallway, and Truman's face abruptly changes—his brow wrinkles and his eyebrows converge in a tight V, indicating his displeasure. Or guilt.

My presence comes between them.

His eyes search mine, and seem to reach a decision. "Nothing will change when we go to Salem. Your heart is my home—if you'll have me, that is."

What does that mean? Does it mean something different in his time than in mine?

My heart is pounding. I barely notice as he stalks across the room to fling open the closet.

"I have much to show you. I won't pretend, it could end badly for both of us."

He reaches inside, extracting a pair of riding breeches, a white shirt and jacket that would have been commonplace on any man in Salem. We were woefully unprepared on our first attempt through the time-door, leaving much to chance. Our clothes haphazard and a great risk.

"Would this do? To go with you, I mean?"

"How? I don't understand?" My head swirls. Could he mean what I think he means?

His smile is wicked, his eyes without a trace of

sadness. They flare with the familiar spark of determination. "I have a friend who works in theater. She's an expert at clothes from every time period."

Staring at the clothes is like a harsh slap. The joy ebbs away as the tentacles of dread threaten, tightening.

In my world, a debilitating fear of the unknown clouds my mind. And a constant helplessness. I have no say in my own existence, no rights, in Salem.

I stare at the clothes with loathing; a jolting reminder of *exactly* who I am.

I stare down at myself, half expecting my shift to materialize.

When he sees what I am to others in my world- someone to be tread upon, ordered around, and who is wholly invisible, will his feelings change?

A young woman unfit to wed, with no wealth, no family. Will he still feel the same, or will he leave me for the gallows?

Impossible. Yet, *this* was the land of impossibilities. Where dreams and reality co-exist.

Not so in Salem. One unforeseen occurrence and one's life is irrevocably altered.

"Yes, the clothes are perfect." I choke out the last word.

He's before me instantly, dropping to one knee.

"Verity, what is it? Your face fell, and your color turned red again. Be honest. If nothing, else, you have to give me that."

I close my eyes as he slides beside me. His fingers cup my cheeks, forcing me to meet his gaze.

I feel so self-conscious. My eyes are abnormal.

No wonder they think me a witch.

His finger drags across his lower lip. I've upset him.

"I know you're afraid. To be frank, I am too. I won't let those paranoid constables harm you. We'll find a way to make it back, and we'll find John, too. Or if the worst happens, and we cannot return…we will stay. And flee."

"It's not that. It's—" My voice cracks again. Anger at my weakness forces out the words.

"Yes, what?"

My hands ball into fists. "Where I am from, I am *nothing*. I am a *possession*, unfit to wed." I walk to his wooden chest that houses the lemon drops.

I pick it up, shake it at him. "This heirloom *holds more worth than I.* I was doomed to serve the rest of my days. I am invisible, seen but never heard."

I swipe my tears with the back of my hand.

Now that I've seen this world, seen what's possible—Salem-life seems a death sentence.

Pain flickers in his eyes, but his face quickly hardens to a stony mask. His fingers tighten a fraction on my cheeks.

"*Listen to me*. I know about being invisible. And *no-one* is *nothing*—to me, anyway." His eyes dart back and forth, searching mine, forging a connection.

He releases me, and his eyes fall to the floor.

He jams them closed and I study the tiny, red capillaries lining his lids.

"I was raised in a string of foster homes and orphanages. Unloved, unwanted, and placed with some terrible families. I knew it wasn't who I was-but there was no escape. No one ever *really looked* at me till I was fourteen years old, when my father adopted me.

He saw me for me. And Verity—*I see you*. Do you understand?"

It's strange when relief finally comes. The icy salve of it, runs through the cracks in my soul. Not healing entirely, but filling them.

He hugs me. "That's better. You're color is lavender again."

His face turns formal, like when he lectures the boys. "We understand how your society worked. Loads of books are written on it. With the hierarchy of who married whom, according to their social status and fortune and what land was to be gained. That doesn't exist here. We are free to marry for love. I know a bad match could doom a family to poverty in your world."

He strides over to the desk and I notice his index finger rubbing his temple.

He hoists up a tottering pile of books, plopping them beside me on the bed.

"I have read so much about Salem, and I feel you need to understand some of the reasons why the trials happened, before returning, Verity."

Somewhere in the back of my head, warning bells clang of the danger in loving someone so fully. I hope my color doesn't betray me again.

"I'm listening."

"Many scholars have studied it. Why so many were hanged, and accused."

The fear oozes out of my cracked heart, and I swallow, not really wanting to hear more. "How many die, True? When I left, only Goody Bishop had been hanged."

"All told, nineteen were hanged, one man pressed

to death, and two dogs. A total of 141 people were arrested."

My hands cradle my head. "John and I were there for the first dog."

He nods grimly. "One of the first reasons historians consider is a condition called mass hysteria, it's one of Ram's favorites." He rolled his eyes playfully, obviously trying to ease the tight look on my face.

I swallow the lump in my throat. "The paranoia began in the Motherland in the year of our Lord, 1641, when King Charles the first, declared it a capital crime to be a witch. The colonies are still under English Law."

It isn't until he sits, and slides his arm around my shoulders that I realize they're shaking. Convulsing, almost.

"I know all about it, love," he murmurs quietly. "Mass hysteria is when a group of people show the same symptoms, sometimes without a physical cause. I can imagine what it was like there, especially for women. No playtime for girls, no using your imagination—it was bound to result in someone acting out."

I give a reluctant nod for him to continue.

"I think I found a better explanation. Some have suggested, perhaps the people of Salem were poisoned… by a mold, called ergot, on the crops. It happens during the rainy season. It's toxic and causes many of the same symptoms—hallucinations, seizures. It would explain many of the behaviors. I imagine it's a combination of these, and just plain malice by some who are jealous of others in their community, or who are trapped in their position, say as a servant?"

Revelations dawn inside my head. Pieces of puzzles falling into place. "Like Mercy…" I think of the witch cake.

"Yes, like Mercy Lewis. Everyone remembers her name, even now."

"Really? That is unbelievable. After all this time?"

He nods. "A man wrote a play called The Crucible with Mercy as a main character. It's quite famous." He stands, pacing again, his finger absently tracing the peppering of reddish stubble on his chin. "Another consideration is an illness called Lyme's disease. The point being, if John is ill, I believe it's physical. We need to get him back here, so we can care for him properly."

"We must go soon. Our clocks do not pass the time equally, and I have no idea what month it is in Salem. My timepiece stopped when I stepped over the bridge."

"Verity, I don't think you have to worry."

His eyes stare again, intense and blue. "When I first met you—well, I couldn't get you out of my head. I searched and searched for you in Salem documents. You are nowhere in history, love. Neither is John."

"What does that mean, Truman?"

"Maybe you are *supposed* to come here, *with me*. To save your souls." He looks thoughtful. "Or for you to save me."

Chapter 20

Truman took one long bracing look at the orphanage.

Possibly his last.

Guilt at leaving Ram and Sunshine burdened with his responsibilities chaffed his conscience.

"Are you ready, love?"

"I am. Truman, remember all the rules. I work for the Putnams, I am a servant. People do not acknowledge me, or touch me."

He stopped her at the entrance to the cornfield and spun her to face him. He gave her a quick kiss. "I hope we aren't there long. I'm quite used to doing that now."

Verity stepped back, eyes roving over his attire one last time. She nodded her approval.

They walked into the corn, winding deeper with every step.

"You are a gentleman, just arrived from Scotland—as we can't change your accent very much, can we?" She brushed his shoulders compulsively, like a servant would her master. "I've heard your attempts at American, they're pathetic. You're arrived in the colonies to start anew and want to employ me, after finding me wandering alone in the fields."

"Yes. Show me one more time where the witch dungeon will be."

He pulled out a 1692 map he'd found online, and it correlated perfectly with Verity's memories of landmarks and homes in Salem Village and Town.

"Here." She pointed several miles away. "The cornfield is close to the Putnam homestead."

"Let's go." He grasped her hand and they trotted through the corn.

Music leached in and around them from another row. And the whispers.

"Do you hear it?" Verity asked. Her mouth screwed up in fear and revulsion.

"Yes. I think the corn personifies your fears, gives them life. It showed me mine." His mind shot back images of his younger self, alone and abandoned.

Something grave passed through her eyes and she gave a little shudder. "Yes, definitely."

He cocked his head. "But the whispers, those are new. Perhaps voices from another time?"

A deep rumble shook the ground beneath their feet, rising like a dog's growl before the bark. Verity froze in place, staring at the dirt.

The ground shook and a fissure erupted, sending Verity's arms pin-wheeling as she grappled for her footing. Her boot-tips jutted half over the edge as she tottered, staring down into a deep crevice in the earth.

Truman lurched forward. His fingers closed on her elbow, yanking her backwards. She tumbled into him, chest heaving. Instinctively he wrapped his arms around her.

Around them, the cornstalks twitched to life. With a deafening thunderclap, a tempest erupted, the howling wind providing a harmony to the background melody of the corn.

The stalks bowed in half, parting like a stage curtain.

He pushed her behind him. Her hand trembled on his back. He could feel her clutching fingers through his shirt.

She whispered in his ear, “Oh my love, what now?”

One image blurred to life on the corn-stage. Verity appeared in a long, elegant white dress; her red hair spiraled to perfection on top of her head. A tiny crown glittered with faux jewels.

“I’m a bride.” Her voice was breathless. “Or a princess.”

He turned to meet her gaze. “That’s a modern dress.”

A crack of thunder scolded him and his attention shot back to the weird stage-show in the corn. The second scene appeared through a filmy mist between the rows. The stalks rattled like skeleton bones.

Verity in her colonial garb, John at her side-as they hastened down a muddy dirt road, toward the corn.

Truman shivered. “It’s choices. It’s showing you choices.”

“As much as I want you—more than anything, ever…my heart will turn to dead stone in my chest without you in my life—I must and shall choose John.”

“Of course you must, he needs you. I would do the same. Perhaps they aren’t either-or.” He squeezed her hand.

The tempest blazed throughout the scenes, cutting a trough down the center of the rows. The dirt flew up on either side of it—as it fell—it suspended. The dirt shimmered madly, changing to deep red flakes. It passed within inches of their feet, and Verity grasped his arm. Snips of sound flew in every direction, making them feel surrounded.

A lion's roar, an elephant's trumpet…a growling—for which he had no name. It seemed to be the conductor of the orchestral timepiece.

"The corn is judge and jury, too. I feel it, thrumming through the air, a vibration. Like my lying sense." His head swung around wildly, his breath quickening with the realizations. "I see spiral colors wrapped around the corn, like a kaleidoscope. It's *every* color, Verity." He squinted, shielding his eyes; the intensity was splitting his head.

"I'm not afraid." Verity said, incredulous. Her face proclaimed her own epiphany. "I think it's a guardian. I was always terrified of the storms back home. This place…gives fear a body. That cyclone's a living fear."

She laughed. It was a disturbed sound, devoid of humor. "And now that I've heard the rest of that song…it makes sense."

Something she said sparked a moment of déjà vu. It was on the tip of his tongue, just out of reach. A thunderclap erupted.

"We have to go. It's open, I knew it would be." Truman pointed to the bright blue sky.

The bluebirds appeared, trilling and weaving between them. They ran down the row, toward the bridge. A second moon was visible at the end of the cornrows.

He grasped her hand. “We have to go.”

Chapter 21

The bridge rumbles as we approach it, clattering up and down as if its old boards are shivering.

This may be your final chance. Say it.

I turn to him, ignoring the crush of fear in my head. “I love you, True.”

“I love you, too. You know it, don’t you?” His eyes mirror my desperation.

“Always.”

He thrusts out his hand, and I wrap his fingers in mine, cherishing every second of his rough skin. We bolt forward, up and over the apex of the bridge. The flexuous door is sticky as we step inside.

Darkness. Spinning.

Then a burst of light so bright, I feel the barbs of it sticking in my eyes. His hand…it’s squeezing mine, tighter. Tighter.

His hand slips down and desperately clutches, crushing my fingertips.

Suddenly, the feel of its gone, and I’m alone. The hornets roar in exultation and I’m weeping.

The fear’s reborn; a live, writhing serpent, waiting to swallow me whole.

The air liquefies at once, as it did the day I first entered his world. The first day of my real life.

Streaming visions of rippling colors appear and disappear at ticking intervals. My hands cover my soaked cheeks and shield my eyes.

Gunfire, women screaming, wailing infants, overlaid with shouts of joy, and sighs of adoration assault my ears. A whirlwind of emotive sound. And under it, the steady drone and buzz of my terror.

My mind is bloated, as if one more sensation enters, it will burst into a million fragments.

My hands burn and I can't stop crying. I bend them into tight fists, clenching the snow. The Salem cold immediately penetrates, sending stinging pangs through my palms, all the way to my fingertips. I will myself upright, but vertigo smacks me back down. I try again, more gingerly, and scan the cornfield. My eyes confirm what my heart refuses to admit.

I am alone.

Anger races through me at the stark hopelessness of this place. It matters not how hard you work, or what good you do. I am sewn into my place in society, with no hope of rescue. I curl into a ball in the snow.

I see John in my head, waiting for me. Hands outstretched. I will just close my eyes for a moment, I lie to myself.

Tears stream, freezing immediately to icy pellets on my cheeks. "Truman? True? Where are you?"

My boot strikes something hard as I struggle to stand.

Truman's journal. I reach down and hug it to my chest as I stumble through the corn, reaching its mouth.

He is nowhere.

But Salem *is*—the Putnam farm stands before me.

Now that I've seen a film, *my* whole world, and its grim reality, appear black and white to me.

The color of Truman's world is already a distant memory, or a page ripped from someone else's story. Perhaps a story I told myself.

The fear is crippling me, weighting my chest, as if I am the one being pressed to death.

Behind me, I hear the girl, Judy, singing. I see her face plainly, not much older than I.

"No. He is here. He must be."

Mercy stands, stock-still on the porch, shaking her head in disbelief. She wrenches open the door to the house and bellows, "Goody Putnam! It's Verity! She's returned!"

Chapter 22

"What! No! Verity!"

Her fingertips slipped away. A pulling sensation rent them apart.

He felt the door thickening under his hands. She was gone—without him. Back to that place. Where she was helpless—had no rights.

He beat on it. Both fists sunk and stuck, like a pliable mold. "She needs me! They will kill her!"

The wind blew past his ear. Voices rode it, like the bluebirds on the morning air. *It isn't time*.

"It bloody well is time!"

He kicked at the bottom of the door, which was hardening into an icy wall. His boot connected, and a crack splintered up to waist level. He wrestled, pulling back his fists, leaning his full weight backward.

He kicked again, and the crack sped up to his hands. It crumbled, releasing them.

The bluebirds squawked, their disharmonious cries crowding out any other sound. Their voices rose and fell, as if mourning. They were everywhere. On every stalk, their shrill trills pierced his ears. It sounded like wailing.

"Can nothing—nothing—in life be easy for me?" He screamed upward, shooting his accusatory gaze into the corn.

His knees gave way, and he stumbled forward. The door popped shut behind him and a sparse rain ticked against the corn-leaves in response.

He automatically started in the direction of the orphanage. Seeing nothing. Hearing only the calls of the bluebirds as they followed him—they moved in one blue, flowing drove, trailing behind his every step.

His legs run, independent of his will.

Sharp leaves cut his cheeks as he whizzes through the winding, muddy paths. Thunder erupts, close enough to vibrate through the stalks.

The birds are wild. Four swoop in his path and he dodges, spinning out of their trajectory. He busts out of the corn to stare at the orphanage. The birds tumble over one another in a mess of feathers and beaks.

Ones at the flock's rear slamming into those in the lead—who are unable to go further.

"They can't leave the corn."

He looks up at his window. Shakes his head once.

"I can't act normal. I can't do it."

Ram appeared on the porch. "Truman—what's going on? Where's Verity?"

The sound of her name sends a surge of rage clawing up his throat. "She's gone."

"Gone where?"

Truman bolts up the porch steps. "Back to Salem."

He swings open the front door, headed for his bedroom. Ram's footsteps hurry behind him. "What happened?"

"I have no bloody idea. It's like it separated us."

"What did?"

Truman whirled. "The corn. The freaking voices in the corn—flying on the wind." He stalked over to the closet, ripping out clothes, shoving them into his rucksack.

"What're you doing? Where're you going? She's gone, man."

"Ram, I can't do this. Pretend like she didn't exist. Like I don't know what's going to happen to her."

"Maybe it wasn't meant to be?"

He screamed. "I don't believe that. Not for a minute! I…can't believe that."

Truman grabbed a sleeping bag, shoving it under his arm.

"What will you do?"

Truman stopped, finally taking in his friend's expression, which had gone as bleak and stark as he felt inside.

"You already have a replacement lined up. Just pretend I'm not here."

"Where—"

"I'm sleeping by the door. I'm not moving till it opens."

* * *

Mistress Putnam's two hands connect with my chest in a hard shove. "Where have you been, Verity? Been in league with the dark one, this many weeks?" Her eyes drop to my middle. "Perhaps you increase with his child, now?"

Her eyes glow with a manic tint. It was the illness, to condemn.

Show no fear.

If they sense a droplet of fear—a judging frenzy, like a shark's bloodlust—will ensue.

"No—I—"

Mistress Putnam lunges, pushing with all her weight behind it. My boot entangles with a foot warmer, and I sprawl.

"Where is John? Does he still live? Please tell me he lives?"

"That warlock be no concern of yours! You might worry about your own neck! It shall snap soon enough."

I wince. "Where is he? Where is he?" I stand up, fist raised, ready to strike. "Where is he, you evil, self-righteous—"

"Verity!" Mercy's trembling voice stops me. "John still lives. He be awaiting trial."

Mistress Putnam strikes her across the cheek.

I raise my fist again, and an iron grip wraps around it. "You…shall not strike you mistress. What has happened to you, girl?" Master Putnam wraps my arm behind my back, till my wrist is between my shoulder blades.

"Ahh!"

"Walk, Verity." He shoves me out into the snow, walking down the road, to town. To my death.

"I do not deserve to die! The devil is not here, master. Listen to me, I have seen the future."

He shoves my arm further up my back and I scream. "Divination. More heresy. Your depravity knows no bounds, girl."

"No—that's not what I mean. I can't see the future—"

I will not go quietly. I now know I will have

rights someday—or my descendants will. I stamp my boot against his toe.

"Ah! You little tartar!"

I feel his fingers loosen. I kick his shin and bolt.

To the corn.

Chapter 23

Truman drops the sleeping bag on the bridge's apex and paces.

"I have to get it together."

He jogs down the planks, heading into the rows. Surely if the wretched door is about to open, he will hear some indication. See the second moon in the sky.

Dusk is falling and his mind keeps taunting him.

What will you do if you cannot see her again?

"I don't know."

The fact is plain, he's forever altered. If he can't save her—he will have to start again.

In everything. His whole life.

He bites the inside of his cheek to keep from screaming.

One bluebird has arrived. It tries to land on his trainer.

"What the—?"

Somewhere far off, the music begins, like a badly tuned radio.

Another bird arrives and another. A row of them are sitting on the corn like a bizarre string of animated party lights.

He follows them, and they sing in approval.

He's back at the bridge. And…

His stomach plummets.

The journal is back at the apex.

He flies up the boards and they shiver, alive once more. His shaking hands crack it open.

~ ~ ~

Oh, my love. Where have you gone? I lost you, along the way. I fear it's over, True. I've escaped. But it's freezing. I have no shelter. My hands…the flesh is changing in the cold. I cannot stay awake. I will not survive the night. Remember me, True. Please—don't give up your search. Love exists. Live your life, give away your heart—but keep a tiny portion, only for me. I've given you all of mine. Know that its last beats sounded your name.

* * *

Hands lift me roughly as someone haphazardly tucks me into his chest. I don't care. I'm so grateful for the warmth. I can no longer feel my left hand. It's like someone cut it from me and cast it aside.

A frantic thought cuts through my dark mind. I peer behind him, looking for the journal.

Tears leak down my cheeks and I smile. "It went through. It went through." My voice is a whisper.

"She's mad." The man carrying me proclaims.

"She knows full well her mind." Constable Corwin. "Don't let her feminine figure addle your mind."

I laugh quietly. I'm no longer afraid of him. I've accepted I'll die. Hate has replaced the fear. I'm not sure which is worse.

"Where is my brother?"

"You will see him soon enough."

We enter Salem Town. Crowds upon crowds follow behind us, trying to catch a glimpse of me.

It's so ridiculous. I, who was once invisible, now cannot hide anywhere. The center of attention.

A house, our destination, looms ahead. I memorize the position of the entrance; the direction, the number of doors.

We enter the house rumored to sit atop the Witch Dungeon.

We follow Corwin's back down a dank staircase.

Manacles, chains, iron. Extra stocks litter the entryway.

My heart shudders as I stare at the prisoner's faces. Their eyes are dead as they've already given away their hope.

"Verity! Oh, laws, Verity!"

"John!"

I am coming apart. My heart falls to pieces. I am crying and ranting and my hands are fluttering as my fingers splay to touch him.

Corwin shoves me into the cell beside him.

My hands instantly grasp both of his. He's crying. I'm crying. I stare so gratefully into those chocolate brown eyes.

"Your joy will be short-lived."

But I barely hear him. His voice is far away and unimportant.

"Oh, John. Just stay close, as close to me as you can."

He snuggles up to the bars between us and I wrap my arms about him as best I can manage.

Somewhere, the jail door clangs shut.

* * *

The journal is strapped to his chest with a piece of leather from the barn he's fashioned into a carrier.

The sleeping bag isn't touching the cold, and his body convulses. He can no longer cry.

He's numb, now. Which is better. His mind's closed off his emotions—keeping them at bay like a rabid dog.

He slips the sleeping bag onto the bridge and crawls inside it. His mind and body are exhausted from the emotional thrill ride of the past twenty-four hours.

He closes his eyes, unsure if he should sleep.

The birds linger unnaturally despite the cold, like bright-blue sentries all around the bridge.

Will the sound of it opening wake me?

He knew he would be unable to keep his eyes open. He was spent.

He stopped fighting, but not listening. Night breezes rose, whipping his hair, breathing across his face.

Whispers, snippets of conversations were like points in space, all around his head, by his feet. Like the disembodied voices have returned.

Fire in the hole!

The baby is gone, Miss.

It isn't time yet.

Jameson, where are you?

The trial be set for the Montagues; two days time.

His eyelids instantly snapped open. He sat straight up, whipping his head toward the door. It shimmered like crusted ice, backlit by sunshine. Sunshine from Verity's side.

Chapter 24

He plunged into the door. It welcomed him, it seemed.

Instead of fractured ice, it now felt like swimming in a warm pool. His body tumbled over and over and he closed his eyes against the force tugging at his face.

He landed—hard, biting his tongue as his face connected with the boards on the other side of the bridge.

Truman patted himself all over, feeling as if disembodied bits of him might still be in the cornfield back home. He was face down in the snow and utterly frozen. He shot to sitting, his head swiveling in every direction. She was nowhere.

"Verity." He whispered her name like a promise.

Screaming for her, a lowly servant girl would only call undue attention to himself.

The nagging fear seemed to mock, *I told you so. Happiness is not for you.*

Pulling out the map, he located Ingersoll's Ordinary and headed immediately in that direction. He quickly dusted the snow off his trousers. He would need immediate shelter against the frigid, falling temperatures.

He located the establishment quickly and slogged,

head down against the wind, as quickly as his feet could carry him through the knee-deep snow.

Upon reaching it, he took a deep breath, pushing the heavy door open with a creak. The dark place smelled musty, and a woman of indeterminate age eyed him warily from behind the bar. Her body was stocky and sturdy and her face a ruddy, healthy complexion—but the lines suggested she'd seen her fair share of sunrises.

"Might I help you, Good sir?"

"Yes, I need lodging."

"You are new to Salem? We do have one open. Might I inquire your name?"

"Truman Johnstone."

She led him to the room, up the staircase without much fuss. A shout sounded from downstairs, and she bustled away. Closing the door after her, Truman placed the single bag he'd brought to the ground. He dropped to his knees, checking for loose floorboards. One lifted up near the bed, and he stowed the small bag beneath it.

The owner most likely knows every loose board in the place, but it gives me peace of mind, just the same.

He walked back down to the common room, where men and women congregated, eating and drinking.

He was about to step outside and head for the Putnam farm, when a snippet of conversation caught his ear.

"When is John Montague to hang, then?"

"Tomorrow at noon. His sister, Verity, has returned. I've heard it won't be long for her, either. As soon as Anne, Jr. saw her, she said Verity's spectral self was tormenting her—pinching her and sitting on the high beams inside the Putnam household. And those little bluebirds were feeding betwixt her fingers."

The woman looked bemused. "Really? I never took Verity for a witch. I mean, her looks are odd, what with that dark red hair and those strange eyes. But she seemed a sweet girl."

"The devil *prefers sweet*. The innocent be susceptible to corruption. Remember, the black man transforms himself into an angel of light! His darkness may not appear frightful; he might have promised her riches. I mean, what chance does a girl like her have? She will serve all of her days, which will be short in number, no doubt."

A cold chill stole up Truman's neck.

I must hurry.

He departed the tavern, back out into the swirling snow.

Walking down the road, he was glad he had enough forethought to bring the handgun. And that Ram had forced him to learn to use one.

He was alone, and felt completely vulnerable walking down the side of the road. An easy target.

Moonlight bounced off the snow, throwing flecks of light into the darkness. It was beautiful. The vast acres glittered like an endless field of crushed diamonds. Farmlands stretched as far as the eye could see, all dowsed in a blanket of white.

It looks like a Currier and Ives painting.

He checked his map after a quarter hour, confirming the house before him was the Putnam's.

He strode to the door and knocked loudly, aware

this was a breach of etiquette with the hour, but unable to contain himself.

Fear for Verity was breathing down his back like a rabid animal.

A man opened the door. "May I help you?"

Truman noted the shotgun in his hand.

"Yes. Are you Good Sir Putnam?"

"Aye."

"I have some business I would like to discuss with you. About your servant, Verity Montague."

Putnam's eyebrow rose in question. He stepped aside to permit him entry to the kitchen, where a fire roared.

Putnam folded his arms. "What about Verity?"

"I'm sure you were aware of her absence of late. I found her, wandering and confused. My household servants nursed her back to health, and I found her quite useful. I'm wanting to purchase her from you."

"That is unfortunate. But Verity is to be tried for witchcraft. They've already taken her into custody. 'Tis a shame, the number of youth corrupted by The Man in Black." He shook his head.

A blast of pain erupted in his chest, leaving behind something more terrifying—a charred space, devoid of feeling. He face fell—he tried to harden it, but his mouth kept twitching. The man's expression gave no indication he was lying. His coloring was a dark yellow, with the characteristic Salem-red line beneath it.

"She is at the jail, then?" He'd managed to keep the tremble out of his voice.

"Yes, The Witch Dungeon, awaiting her trial."

He stepped out of the house, back into the snow

and trotted until he was sure he was out of sight of the house.

He broke out into a flat out sprint.

* * *

Think man. Don't feel.

His head felt thick and stupid, stuffed with the white clouds floating overhead. He'd considered a million scenarios during his totally sleepless night. Terror kept choking his wits, suffocating rational thoughts.

It was almost noon, he'd been walking since sun-up, trying to devise a plan. He'd arrived back at Ingersol's, and decided it was as good a place as any to begin.

The tables were filling up, so he sat at the bar.

He focused on the people in the room, listening intently, watching their expressions.

His senses gunned into overdrive. He absently felt his fingers worrying Verity's locket, hidden in his pocket. His eyes darted from table to table.

A man's mouth trembled, with a tic, "I'll pay ya' next week Charles, for certain." *Lie.*

A woman's eyes fluttered in flirtation at the large man beside her. "No, I'm not married, good sir." Her brow crinkled into tight, lined, rows of flesh. *Liar.*

Stop it. Block them out. Verity, oh God help me, Verity.

He eavesdropped on snippets of conversations, searching for the names he needed—Constable Corwin being his prime interest.

He racked his brain to remember days and dates

of the witch trials. He knew most of the hangings occurred in summertime. He wished fervently for his BlackBerry and a World Wide Web connection to fact-check.

He fingers stroked the locket in his hand, like a worry stone. So it was back to this? Only *dreaming* of her—not *having* her. White-hot anger colored his face and he ground his teeth.

No, I will die trying. I can't live with only the memory of her.

He motioned for the bar keep to come near. "Is that Constable Corwin, then?"

She raised a suspicious eyebrow. "Yes. 'ho's askin'?"

An idea struck him. "Johnstone. I'm from Andover, sent by the court to record the names of the accused, along with their symptoms, and report back. We're having a spot of trouble ourselves, and are comparing the afflicted in affected towns."

Her face blossomed into a smile, removing ten years from it. "All right, then. Constable Corwin?"

His name tasted like lemons, tangy but bitter in his mouth.

The man across the room looked wary, but rose and walked toward them.

For the first time in his life, Truman fully focused on his 'difference'. Most of his life was spent blocking it, just living with it, but he was desperate for any small advantage that would lead him to Verity.

The man's color was an odd combination. A carrot pious orange on the outside, with an under-layer he felt to be a forest colored confusion. Only traces of the Salem-red appeared.

Of course not. He controls the outcome for so many lives, here. Who will live, who will die.

The barmaid introduced him, and stated his purpose to the man.

The constable didn't look wholly convinced. Truman was certain the man would ferry a representative to Andover to check his story, the second he was out of sight.

"So, you are recording the ailments then?"

"Yes, sir. And if you do not mind, Constable, I would like to begin as soon as possible."

Emotional waves exuded from his every pore, and Truman sensed the partial distrust—but not outright. His every move was being evaluated.

He honed his ability, the focus narrowing to a tunnel, ending in Corwin's face. The single lift of the man's eyebrow ricocheted off the inside of his brain, emitting a flowing trail of geometric patterns, and colored emotions.

He reeled with the impact, and gritted his teeth.

Sequences appeared, in the man's dialogue, and his mind shifted, analyzing Corwin's movements and automatically categorizing them, like a mental spreadsheet, against every other person and similar emotion he'd ever seen or felt.

He swallowed hard, he felt like a bloody computer. He pictured a stream of analog numbers spiraling on a desktop screen. Only his were minute mannerisms.

"Good sir?"

Truman popped out of his absorption. "Yes, let's begin immediately."

Chapter 25

As Corwin led Truman down the dank stairwell, Truman's heart beat wildly in his chest. *The witch dungeon.* It did exist, after all. Historians debated its very existence.

The stench burned his nose as they descended the rickety staircase. Large, wet stones echoed their footfalls as a rat swept past in his peripheral vision. His boots tramped through an inch of water. He shivered, imagining all the diseases swimming in the fetid pools, ready and waiting to germinate in their unwilling human hosts.

The prison cells were abundant and diverse. Some were larger, housing several people. Others were upright, as small as telephone booths; requiring the person to choose between standing in perpetuity or a cramped, crouched squat.

Those are the coffin cells I read about. For the poor.

He shivered, imagining the depression of imprisonment there—day in, day out. The injustice, awaiting your death for a crime you didn't commit. And here were the faces of the damned, staring back at him with huge, hollow eyes.

The colors. He swallowed hard. They were a tide

of hopelessness. Like the place was a vacuum, sucked completely devoid of positive energy.

No wonder so few survived—the diseases, the complete inability to sleep.

He swallowed, hoping he wouldn't find out first-hand.

Honing in on his ability-the room thrummed with colored emotions and patterns, making him instantly ill with vertigo. He battled it, trying to filter and channel it, reading one person at a time.

"Are you well, sir?" Corwin was eyeing him again.

"Yes, fine. The smell."

"Oh, yes."

"I will leave you to your work. There is a jailer outside the door at all times."

"Thank you." He dipped his head in a little bow of thanks, hoping the gesture wasn't over the top. He hadn't had much time to study the manners of the period.

Without the distraction of Corwin, his discrimination instantly zeroed in on Verity. Her cheek pressed against the stones, either asleep or unconscious. Her colored blinked like a strobe light between her normal gentle lavender and a blinding red fear.

All eyes in the room watched him warily. Their colors spoke one communal feeling—*enemy.*

Despite Verity's small stature, her legs pathetically jutted out of the coffin cell. He felt the lump rise in his throat. He swallowed it, determination setting his jaw.

Gently shaking her boot, he tried to rouse her.

"Miss? Miss?"

A young man in the next cell turned a slow, sunken gaze toward him. His ashen complexion and black circles underlining his eyes, gave him a look of the walking dead.

"Do not you touch her." His hand launched out of the cell, grasping Truman's collar, shaking him.

"John, stop. It's all right." Verity's eyes opened, looking both terrified and hopeful.

John dropped his hand and nodded, never taking his fervent gaze from Truman's hand, still clasping her boot. Truman ordered his hand to release her. He pictured grabbing her through the bars and kissing her. He swallowed instead.

"I'm here from the constable's office in Andover. I need to talk to you about when your illness began, and whether or not the dark man has presented himself to you, in spectral form, to sign his book?"

Truman conducted approximately five interviews, taking the histories of the accused. Verity's eyes burned his back as he moved from cell to cell.

Finally after an hour, the door to the outside opened.

"Time is up, sir." One of the guards stood with hands folded at the entrance. "We need to feed the prisoners."

"Yes, all right then."

Truman dropped a note to the ground, immediately stepping on it with his boot. As he turned to go, he slid it toward Verity's cell with his pivot.

It read, *Tonight.*

Chapter 26

Truman choked down his dinner in the Ordinary, while several women batted their eyelashes, overtly flirting with him.

The dark room felt too close and stale. Too many smells overwhelmed his sensitive perceptions.

His stomach lurched as one woman leaned in provocatively, reeking of alcohol. "You sure you won't join us, sir? We love to show hospitality to new folks in town." She smiled invitingly.

"That is very gracious, but I'm quite tired. Perhaps another time?"

He struggled to keep the food down, his stomach roiling as his eyes continually swept the room.

Not to sup, however, would arouse suspicion. The Innkeeper monitored his every move. No doubt, her watchful eye was under the orders of Constable Corwin, who awaited his fact checker's return from Andover, to see if Truman was whom he claimed to be.

His time was running out. When the courier returned, the sands of his hour glass were empty.

Angling his way through the dinner crowd, he headed upstairs, intent on getting to his room. On the steps, the bar keep stopped him.

"Can I get you anything Good Sir? Are you to retire?"

"No, thank you. I'm off to bed. The trip has made me weary."

The constant stream of rewording in his head, from modern Scottish-American to colonial dialect was exhausting. His slow replies made him look dim-witted as there was a pregnant pause before every response.

Verity was right—he was a terrible actor. The mere thought of her sent another wave of anxiety crashing on his head. *Every* thought was of her, who was he kidding?

"Good night, Good sir."

He walked past the doors on either side, wondering about the people behind them.

No one was safe here—all potential death row victims.

He reached his door and entered the sparse room with a sigh.

Sitting on his bed, Truman listened till the sounds of the Ordinary died away, and no footfalls could be heard on the stairs outside. His fingertips thrummed on his kneecaps-his nervous tension rose, scratching at his gut like an impatient rodent.

He checked his pocket watch. "Finally. I can't wait any longer. She's so close."

Wrenching open the floorboards, he extracted the rucksack. He opened it, checking the contents.

A compass, a few items for barter, if necessary, and chloroform. Ram had weaseled some out of his chemist friend, convincing him it was for rat experiments at his psychology lab. He didn't have much—he'd have to use it judiciously.

Another pistol, loaded. A carton of ammunition. Ram had taught him to use a gun after coming to the U.S. Living in the woods, with no one around for miles—Ram felt it essential they were able to defend themselves. To protect the boys.

A flashlight—also a potential heap of trouble if it were discovered.

I hope I don't set off some timeline continuum warp if someone sees it.

"This is mental. I will probably be tried as a witch alongside her for my *spectral* light source."

Truman rose, staring out the window. The night outside was utter blackness, no streetlights, very few homes lit. The whole of the village died after sundown. Nothing like night at home—where the reassurance of light was never far off.

He returned to checking the contents.

A baton, which Ram called a nightstick.

Sweat beaded on his brow.

If I'm caught skulking around downstairs, they will know I'm up to something.

In this century, people did not go out at night unless they had a specific purpose.

Opening the door a crack, he peered down the hall, and debated the staircases. He decided. The back one, as dealing with a few servants was preferable to explaining himself to any lingering patrons.

He crept out, his heartbeat so loud, he swore its echo followed him down the hallway.

The back staircase creaked with his every footstep, making the sweat trickle down his back, despite the bitterly freezing temperatures outside.

He paused at the mouth of the stairwell, listening intently behind the door. From the sound of it-only one person worked in the kitchen. He cracked the door a slit, and spied a young woman tidying up around the fire.

She shoveled coals from the fire into a foot warmer, and heaved it up.

He held his breath. *Was she going to come up these stairs?*

He exhaled through his teeth as she pushed open the door and lugged it into the eating area.

Moving swiftly, he darted out the back door and sprinted in the direction of the witch dungeon.

* * *

Truman arrived at the witch-dungeon with surprisingly little fuss, using the flashlight only when it became utterly too black to see his own feet on the ground before him.

Several small lights glowed in the windows of the building, reminding him of glowering, evil eyes. The dungeon was secluded in the lower basement of the building. When researching the Salem Trials, Truman remembered reading the remnants of it were not discovered till many years later.

But Verity had known of it, so she was able to describe its location.

He circled the building, searching for the most likely entry point. He decided on a nondescript door at the back of the building.

To his surprise, it was unlocked. However, this most likely meant somewhere in the house, someone was awake and standing guard.

As the door creaked open he immediately spied the familiar door, behind which was concealed the stairs leading to the witch dungeon.

Moving as quietly as possible, he stole down the staircase. Massive stones lined the walls, and the familiar musty smell of fetid water stung his nostrils. His eyes watered and he swiped them with the back of his hand.

Colors swirled through the air of the stairwell; remnants of emotional energy from the prisoners below were so violent, they refused to be contained within the thick stone prison walls. If their owners could not escape, they would.

Gritting his teeth, he fought against the despair and anger welling inside him. He wondered at the atrocities human kind was capable of committing. The majority of those housed below were *ill*, mentally or physically, not witches. Most were poor victims—the outcasts of society; or the opposite, people so blessed, others coveted their lives.

Outcasts like he, and Verity, and John. Persecuted because of their differences. It disgusted him.

Who of us is so worthy, to decide what is normal and what is not? To decide who's soul is worth saving?

He reached the bottom of the stairs, listening for the jailer. One man had his back to him, his head half-lolling in sleep.

Across the room, another doorway was visible. A man's foot stuck out in the middle of the entry as he relaxed in a chair.

He launched himself at the closest one, smacking

the back of his head with the baton. The man crumpled to the floor. Truman stepped over him.

Hurrying to the entryway, his eyes spied the ring of keys. They hung on a ring beside the guard's head. This sentry half snored as well, his body draped over the desk. Truman debated the club or the chloroform, deciding on the latter.

He poured a small amount on the rag, holding it far from his face.

Crossing the room in a tic, he clamped it over the man's mouth. The guard's hands clawed wildly at the air, and their glance connected for a brief second till the lights of consciousness extinguished in his eyes. He slumped forward to the desk.

The captives in the dungeon were frantic now.

Screams and shouts were filling the air.

"Be quiet!" Truman chastised. "You will never get out if the whole town is awake."

"Truman, I cannot believe it. I thought all was lost." Verity grasped John's hand through the cell bars.

Truman's hand fumbled, trying to locate the correct key. Shouts echoed down the stairwell. Reinforcements were coming.

There were at least thirty on the ring. He'd never find it in time.

A stampede of footsteps barreled down the stairwell.

"Tru-man!" Verity's eyes were manic. "You must go. Leave us! There is no other way!"

"No. I can't."

John's eyes grew uncharacteristically focused. "Truman, you must. Go. Run."

His panic stuttered his thoughts, and he looked

wildly around for an escape. One small window was his only hope. He bolted toward it, scrambling upward. As it slammed shut, he heard the voices of the constables and the screams of the prisoners gel into one sickening sound.

He bolted toward the ordinary.

* * *

Truman paced, not seeing anything. Shockwaves of adrenaline pulsed from his heart and mushroomed down his arms, making them weak.

"What am I going to do?"

He crammed his eyes shut, and slid down the wall, clenching into a tight ball.

The sun was rising and Verity's life was setting.

Hundreds of scenarios played out behind his eyes, all ending with him hanging as well.

So he shot his way to her at the gallows? He couldn't fight off an entire town. *He had a pistol, not a semi-automatic rifle.*

A tapping sound shattered his reverie.

A bluebird sat on the windowsill, its beak pecking on the glass.

Truman stared. It stared back.

"What the…"

He *swore* it was waiting for him. How had it gotten out of the corn?

It tilted its head, in question? Its eyes looked deep, not superficial, like many animals.

He gasped. It had a color. Blue, what else?

He barked a laugh.

It flew away and he flew down the stairs after it.

People were heading toward Gallow's Hill, whispering.

"Who is it today?"

"John and Verity Montague."

"Really? I thought she was dead already?"

He ground his teeth together, speeding up so as not to hear the rest.

He squinted, staring at the sky. The sun was bright today.

The blue bird hovered above the migrating crowd, never getting too far ahead.

Then he saw her. And John.

His hands shook so violently he shoved them in his pockets.

And felt them. The lemon drops were still there. On a whim, he'd shoved them in; it had felt wrong, somehow to leave them in his time.

He counted them with his fingers. *Ten.*

At last count, he'd had only five.

Verity held John's hand, and he could see her whispering to him, keeping him calm. All of his perception tuned on Verity. Her face a mess of emotion. John's eyes were downcast, and he rocked in place. His senses honed, he could read her lips.

"Remember John. We'll be with mama and papa, soon. It's just like going to sleep. When you wake, it will be like nothing you've ever seen."

"Will it hurt?"

Truman's whole body quaked. A sadness so large, it teetered on madness, reeled through his mind.

His teeth gritted, as a fierce, protective urge demanded action.

He thrust his hand inside the bag, grasping the

pistol.

The bird flew to the front of the crowd, to the bottom of the knoll. He followed it, angling his way through the expectant onlookers.

Truman's throat constricted so tight, his breathing came in gasps now.

"Verity Montague. You and your brother be charged with witchcraft. How do you plead?"

"Not guilty." Her voice rang, clear as a bell across the crowd.

A ruckus at the front of the knoll shifted the crowd's attention. Several girls fell to the ground at the sound of Verity's voice.

"Not guilty. Not guilty." The gruesome trio, Anne Jr., Abigail and Mercy, mocked in unison, in their sing-song voices.

"You are condemned to die. May God have mercy upon your soul."

Truman slid the gun out, concealing it beneath the bag, ready to aim at the hangman's leg.

A tug at his sleeve bade him look down.

A tiny girl held out her hand, waving a yellowing parchment.

"It's from her." She pointed up at Verity.

He almost pocketed it, but the bluebird swooped beside him, landing square on his boot.

He opened it.

~ ~ ~

One who condemns the soul to die,
To him, all the pretty birds must fly,
His breath, like lemon, sour-sweet,
It holds the key, him to defeat.

~ ~ ~

Revelations sparked, then ignited in his head, in a split second. Reaching into his pocket, he grasped a handful of the lemon drops, and turned, running toward the corn.

He cocked his arm, pelting them into the rows. Several people turned toward the commotion, including the hangman. His hand stayed on the noose.

The victrola music crackled to life, filtering out of the corn.

"And the dreams…"

Nothing was happening. His mind whirled, searching desperately for something, anything, that might help them.

He spun toward the crowd, they gave no indication of hearing the music. Most eyes were still staring fixedly at the gallows.

He turned to the knoll. Verity's eyes caught his.

Her full lips mouthed the words, "That you dare to dream."

An *explosion* of blue erupted from the corn. Thousands of bluebirds barreled out of its depths, shrieking and screaming, dive-bombing the crowd of villagers.

The air was rife with wings and beaks. The birds congested the space between the villagers so thickly they were frozen in place, afraid to move. Their trilling was deafening. A bizarre, sweet-sounding song called from their tiny bodies.

Truman gaped, no one was being hurt. They were merely a distraction.

John was covering his ears, rocking in place as Verity's hands reached out to him.

Somewhere in the corn, he heard the low drone of

voices rise, young and old, feral and calm.

Another maelstrom of feathers bloated the air as a second cavalry hit. He saw Corwin and Hathorne surrounded by a revolving tornado of birds, which pecked and pulled, every time they tried to move.

"This surely is the work of The Man in Black! Hang her!" Corwin screamed.

Truman bolted, pistol drawn, storming the hill.

The hangman was swatting at one hundred birds, which pushed him in a wall of flapping wings, away from the nooses. He tripped, and rolled down the hill inside a swirling, undulating mass of feathers.

He scrambled to the top, briefly squeezing her hands, and then wresting the noose from her neck. He moved swiftly to John.

"Oh, T-Truman."

"No time, love. We have to move."

Villagers were screaming over the shrieking birds. Some tried to clamber up the hill, only to be beaten back by the bluebirds.

"She is getting away! The Witch! Seize her!"

They bolted for the corn, holding hands in a chain.

* * *

"Verity, we have to get to the corn. Run faster!"

They ran, as fast as they could, half-dragging John between them.

Barks sounded in the night.

"Not the dogs again. John, you must *run*!"

The barks seemed to have woken a primal fear in John, his eyes churning. He launched himself into a gangly half-lope, half-run beside them.

Weaving through the rows, the dogs' clipped barks were mere rows behind.

"They have to be in here somewhere!"

After what seemed an eternity, the longest minutes of his life-the bridge came into view.

Grasping hands, the trio bolted up its planks.

"Please, open. Please, ruddy open," he heard himself chanting.

Another moon materialized on the other side, and he nearly wept.

The three busted through the gelatinous door. Lights in every hue flickered, coupled by the perception of spiraling down the center of a cyclone funnel. The time stream whipped across his face, contracting and relaxing at regular intervals.

"Don't let go!" Verity screamed. He could no longer see her, but felt her grip tighten on his hand. She sounded miles away. And so terrified. He remembered landing in the corn alone, and crushed her hand in his.

They landed with a thud on the other side, in a dog-pile of arms and legs.

Verity shrieked, her brown and hazel eyes wide with horror.

Dogs crouched at the gelatinous doorway, snarling and biting at it. Fangs bared, hackles raised, they stared with malice at the trio sprawled on the ground.

"They can see us," Truman marveled.

A group of men appeared behind them, apparently seeing nothing. They stumbled around in confusion, yelling at one another in the chaos.

"They were just here!"

"That is bloody impossible! This cornfield is bewitched by the Man in black, no doubt!"

They whistled the dogs back off the bridge.

The three sat on the ground, huddled together in relief. John and Verity's chests heaved in unison, desperately clutching one another.

Truman swiped his face with the back of his hand, and bowed his head. Giving thanks for perhaps only the third time in his life. Perhaps there was some justice in the world.

"Let's get back to the house," he said, gently grabbing each of them by an elbow. "I want to get out of the corn." The music seemed to mourn, now.

Verity shot him a tear streaked gaze. "Listen to it. So sad. That's not your song."

He cocked his head. "No. It must mean something. And it cannot be good."

They took off at a trot down the row leading toward the orphanage.

Chapter 27

Weaving down the rows, Truman was flat out running. An unpleasant apprehension was mounting and corresponding tracks of feelings, surging in his head, were doing miniscule calculations. They were not safe yet.

Like a curtain call with the words spoken in his mind-the path ahead went black, as if night had fallen.

"Like when darkness followed the Egyptians in the Bible," he murmured.

John nodded. "Y-Yes, one of the ten plagues."

Truman laughed nervously. "We better not be the Egyptians. I'm shooting for Israelite under the circumstances."

A cannon's boom shot through the night. A hissing noise rent their ears as a projectile's arc whizzed toward them, growing louder and louder.

"Get down!" Truman screamed.

A cannonball blasted through the curtains in the corn, landing not twenty feet away; its force taking out an entire row in one destructive swoop.

They bolted past the open curtain, sprinting away toward the center of the maze.

Truman yelled over his shoulder, not breaking stride. "The maze must open to other time periods besides yours, Verity."

The orphanage was in sight now, about ten minutes of winding rows away. Verity's fingers grasped his arm, slowing him.

From every corner of the corn, gruesome scenes raged—like a thousand drive-in movie screens, plastered into the corn.

To the north, he plainly recognized Revolutionary War uniforms, as they whizzed past the open window in time.

To the south, a huddle of children screamed in terror. A locust swarm gathered, so thick and tight, they disappeared beneath its undulating multitude.

To the west, a beautiful girl, with raven-black hair, played a cello. Tears streaked her full cheeks as she stared lovingly up at the moon.

"Who are they?"

"We have been brought together for more than true love." Her mismatched eyes were troubled and filling again. "I feel certain of it."

"Someone is coming! It's from the direction of the south door, run!" Truman shouted at them.

Verity grasped John's hand and they flew through the stalks winding toward the orphanage.

Truman shot glances over his shoulder trying to get a glimpse of the attacker.

He stopped, giving them a lead, and slipped into a particularly thick cluster of stalks, waiting.

A young man, blond and handsome, dressed in what he estimated to be 18th century attire, charged toward him.

When the man's foot struck the ground before him, Truman launched into the air, tackling him.

Rolling through the corn, he grappled to restrain the stranger. The man was younger than him, and a little thicker-but the sheer adrenaline force surging through him gave him the advantage.

Straddling him, he shot a punch across the man's jawbone.

It was then he noticed the colors outlining his person, so similar to the residents of Salem—deep azure blue, outlined in red.

Fear. Is he frightened of me?

Truman's computer-like mind launched without his permission into a whirlwind analysis of the man's expression. A database of micro-facial patterns registered, flowing toward him in a colored queue, and exploding into a tight analysis, culminating in an intuition.

The man's blue eyes widened, and Truman saw the familiar emotions which were all tagged by color and geometric shape. His analysis computed in ten seconds.

He paused with his fist cocked in the air.

"Please sir. The-the wind sent me. I desperately need your help." He swallowed. "And I know that sounds mad."

Truman's mouth dropped open, and he slumped to the ground beside him.

He reached out to touch him. The man faded, like a photograph. First losing his color, turning black and white, and then to nothing.

John and Verity reappeared, in time to see his disintegration.

They stared at the spot, unmoving. John dropped to his knees, feeling around on the ground.

"I, I don't understand," she finally said.

A deep, mournful call of a cello surrounded them.

A thunderous crack shook the corn.

The whirling dervish appeared, and from it the whispers. "He will return. It's a time track. A replaying of history, if you will."

"What can we do?"

The whirlwind circled Verity. "She knows."

"To much whom is given, much shall be expected." Her eyes searched mine, clear and open.

"He will return. Will you help him?"

Truman stared around him. The scenes were fading into the night, like a fizzling fireworks display. Popping out one after the other. Till the night was black, and quiet.

The only remaining sound was…the bluebirds.

His father's words returned to his head, *Your intellect doesn't matter. It is what you choose to do with it.*

He knew. They were all chosen, bound together through a thread in time to help those who could not help themselves.

Verity eyed him, but her expression left no doubt.

He took Verity's hand, and after a moment, hugged John to his other side.

"Yes. What do we need to do?"

Epilogue

One year later, October.

I walk out onto the porch and stare at the barnyard. To say this day will be hectic, is an understatement. The sun is burning off the morning mist, but I shiver a little and wrap my sweater more tightly around my shoulders. I drink in the cornucopia of fall leaves that litter the yard. The past year has been the best of my life, and it's going to end.

I turn to see my brother sitting on the rocker. I flinch. He's so quiet, he blends into the porch furniture.

"Hi, John. How's it going with Edward?"

The autistic boy looks up at me with the mention of his name. He signs 'hello'.

"That is wonderful, that he said hi to me on his own. You are doing a marvelous job."

John is not going with me, and for that, I'm glad.

"Thank you sister." John's eyes shine with pride.

He belongs here, where he is safe, and finally has other people who love him as much as I.

Ram pokes his head out the door. "Come on, Edward, John. We have lots to do today. The Festival starts at noon, and we are nowhere near ready."

Shouts and laughter seep into the barnyard as Ram opens the front door wider.

"Verity? You all right?" Ram asks. His eyes flick to the corn with a resigned expression. The clock is ticking. He and I have come to terms. We understand each other now.

"Yes. I'm just going to find True, and then I'll be right in to help." I smile at him.

I leave the porch and head across the barnyard.

The cornfield towers above me, tall and green. I planted sunflowers at its mouth—perhaps to combat my own fear of the place. The result is a pleasing contrast of yellow flowers and black faces against the leafy green maze door.

A map of the new maze is affixed to a wooden podium at the entrance.

I stare at it, tracing the steps to the bridges in the maze with my finger.

Where will we go this year? Will it be the same? Will that young man truly be waiting? And the voices? I've entered the stalks a million times, and it's quiet. The music is gone.

"But the birds are here." I smile up at a flock of them. They perch on the corn, watching, as always.

The sound of hoof beats cut through my musing. Truman angles the appaloosa around the hay bales, stopping in front of me. The sun glitters off the russet stubble on his cheeks.

My stomach drops a little, just looking at him. I know it's dangerous to love someone so much. But I have no choice in the matter. Time hasn't dampened my desire.

He extends a hand to me.

"Ram is looking for you."

"One ride," Truman says, glancing at the house like a boy escaping his chores.

I grin and shove my foot in the stirrup, throwing myself behind him.

His foot gives the mare a nudge and we're flying. The wind streams through my hair like a crimson kite and I laugh.

I squeeze him and kiss his neck. Make every moment count, is the way I live now.

He slows the horse at the north mouth of the maze, and speaks quietly, so I have to strain to hear him.

"It's almost time." My arms are around his waist, and his thumb caresses my fingers. "We promised we'd return."

I stare at the corn. If I die, I have had a year of being loved perfectly—which some will never experience. I lift my face to the sun.

"I'm ready."

Author's Notes:

Proposed Causes of the Salem Witch Trials

Many theories have been explored with regard to the etiology of the Salem Trials-mass hysteria, class rivalry and strict Puritan behavior requirements to name a few.

Children in Salem, most especially girls, had no creative outlet. Pretending and play were discouraged, and the tasks they were taught—sewing, cooking—provided no physical activity. Whereas boys were given the opportunity to hunt and fish which, at the very least, provided them with exercise.

Women in particular had a difficult lot. If one was orphaned from the many Indian skirmishes of the time, the girl was destined for a hard life as a servant to a wealthier family.

Mass hysteria is defined as a group of people's belief they are suffering from a common ailment (often imagined) and occurs during extreme periods of stress.

Salem has often been cited as one such historical occurrence of the disorder.

Another fascinating explanation suggested by Linnda Caporael, a behavioral scientist, was that the people of Salem might have been poisoned with ergot, a mold that collected on the crops during the rainy season. Interestingly, it has been suggested ergot might have also been the root cause of the character in Shakespeare's THE TEMPEST, who suffered convulsive fits.

The people and animals (dogs) would ingest the grains and suffer the consequences. The witch-cake, mentioned in the book, is a documented event. The drug L.S.D. is actually a derivative of ergot. And the symptoms of the afflicted girls, the odd skin sensations, hallucinations, convulsions, and delirium could be readily explained by the effects of this drug.

Of course, in some of the cases, outright maliciousness and class jealousy was undoubtedly a cause. The strict social norms of the time were a catalyst for more creative or active minds to act out. Continuous insistence on uniform behavior, and no free time for children exacerbated the girls' attention-seeking behaviors. All claims of witchcraft were taken seriously, including those posed by children as well as adults. So all that was needed was a finger pointed in your direction, and you might be next to swing on gallows hill.

**Lord's Prayer*—Many people in Salem were convicted for witchcraft for the inability to state the Lord's Prayer correctly. So if one was under the effects of ergot poisoning with its muscle contractions, or born with a congenital stutter, or perhaps a learning disability…and were requested to perform this task-they were doomed.

**Coffin Cells*—According to the historians at the Witch Dungeon Museum, the very existence of the dungeon was disputed at first, but the site was unearthed during a construction project, later in history. Coffin cells were the size of telephone booths, and were impossibly cramped. The conditions of the dungeon were dank and wet; a perfect breeding ground for disease. Many did perish in the dungeons while awaiting their fate. All of the prisoners, even if released, were required to pay for their room and board while held. This left poor folks without family incarcerated indefinitely. Wealthier families were also afforded more spacious cells.

**Pressing*—The act of pressing, or crushing an individual with massive weight, occurred to one man during the hysteria of the trials. According to the history tours in Salem, Giles Corey, a difficult, belligerent man, felt all his years of toiling would not be passed on to his heirs if he falsely confessed to witchcraft. He needed only to confess and he would go free; however, his land would be forfeit. Therefore, Corey refused to enter a plea, and they sentenced him to be pressed to death.

**Synesthesia*—A condition in which normally separate senses combine. Sight may mingle with sound, taste with touch, etc. The senses are cross-wired. For example, when a digit-color synesthete sees or just thinks of a number, the number appears with a color film over it. A given number's color never changes; it appears every time with the number. Synesthesia can take many forms. A synesthete may sense the taste of chicken as a pointed object. Other synesthetes hear colors. Still others may have several senses cross-wired.

Estimates of the frequency of synesthesia range from 1 in 250,000 to 1 in 2,000. People with synesthesia are 6 times more likely to be female than male. Most synesthetes find their unusual sensory abilities enjoyable.

People with synesthesia often report that one or more of their family members also have synesthesia, so it may in at least some cases be an inherited condition.

It may be that synesthesia arises when particular senses fail to become fully independent of one another during normal development. According to this school of thought, all babies are synesthetes. Synesthesia can be induced by certain hallucinogenic drugs and can also occur in some types of seizure disorders.

The words synesthesia is a hybrid of Latin and Greek—the Latin syn- (together) + -esthesia, from the Greek aisthesis (sensation or perception). MedicineNet.com

**Synesthesia* is a cognitive difference, well documented and quite real. Synesthaetes throughout history were classified as insane. This should not surprise us though, as almost any illness that was not clearly understood was seen as possession or the like.

Many people hid their ability, and in 1812 a scientific paper was written on the subject. Most likely only medical personnel felt comfortable discussing their synesthesia for fear of repercussions.

It can occur in so many different forms—some see shapes and colors from music, others taste different words or individual sounds. Some taste shapes or hear shapes. There are a myriad of combinations.

It seems as individual as the person. For some, there are so many cross-wirings going on that overstimulation can occur while in crowded settings, but for others, with only one overlap in senses, it is quite manageable. Even enjoyable.

Synesthesia does not have defined rules, it is as subjective as the person it inhabits. Meaning the letter K may appear green for one person, yellow for another etc.

The ability to see colors around people IS a documented phenomenon.

I had the privilege to interview some persons about synesthesia, and how it affected their lives. Many were unaware they were unique, thinking everyone thought in the same manner as they did. Once they were aware, they became self-conscious, only sharing it with trusted family or friends.

**Lives Cut Short*—Near the Peabody Essex Museum in Salem, M.A., one may find the Salem Witch Memorials. Each of the park's twenty stone benches represents persons hanged for witchcraft. Several of the stones contain chiseled quotes from the victims, including the haunting words, "God knows I am not guilty." Some of the quotes are cut off, signifying the lives cut short.

Definitions:

**Maleficia*—Any malicious acts which were contributed to witches and sorcerers in past times that were believed to cause harm or death to humans, animals or crops.

From Mimi.hu website.

**Ordinary*—The name for the public eating and drinking place in Salem, Massachusetts in 1692.

**Tactile Defensiveness*—is a disorder where the

skin is responding abnormally, either too sensitive or not sensitive enough, most likely due to poor nerve conduction.

**Occupational Therapy*—Occupational Therapy is about understanding the importance of an activity to an individual, being able to analyze the physical, mental and social components of the activity and then adapting the activity, the environment and/or the person to enable them to resume the activity. Occupational therapists would ask, "Why does this person have difficulties managing his or her daily activities (or occupations), and what can we adapt to make it possible for him or her to manage better and how will this then impact his or her health and well-being?" Wikipedia

References:

The Salem Witch Trials, Marilyn K. Roach Taylor Trade Publishers, 2002

Historical Tours of Salem Massachussetts—Author's Notes

Peabody Essex Museum Tours—Author's Notes

About the Author

Born and raised in western Pennsylvania, Brynn Chapman is the daughter of two teachers. Her writing reflects her passions: science, history and love—not necessarily in that order. In real life, the geek gene runs strong in her family, as does the Asperger's syndrome. Her writing reflects her experience as a pediatric therapist and her interactions with society's downtrodden. In fiction, she's a strong believer in underdogs and happily-ever-afters.

You can read more of her weird ramblings at www.brynnchapmanauthor.com.

Made in the USA
Lexington, KY
16 October 2018